Chapter 1

September's ocean breeze brushed Mizzou's
sandy hair. The bitter air, thick with salt, congealed
his spittle into a globule that stuck to the roof of his
mouth like peanut butter, yet he managed somehow
to launch a golden goober toward pavement.
Struggling against furious wind, he closed the heavy
rear doors of Fly By Night Van Lines' straight-truck
#123.

A squat man stomp, stomp, stomped his fat,
greasy boot on the gas pedal. "Come on, now,
Philip," he mumbled, spitting each word out
between the perfect teeth that bit an unlit, crooked
cigar. The squat man called his stogy a "cherry
cheroot." Mizzou called it "stink-breath death."

Face red, Mizzou's exasperation showed and he
implored, if not to the door then to himself: "Move,
you devil." Upon command, the wind died and the
door slammed shut. Had he not gripped the handle
tightly, Philip Mizzou would have been pitched to
the ground. Despite his height, however, Mizzou
was coordinated, so the lurch only startled but did
not drop him.

Tasks complete, another job done, Mizzou parked
his size twenty-two, double-wide, pontoon boots on

1

the truck's floor. With gears popped into low, the ancient big-rig sputtered along The Embarcadero toward Highway 101. On the open road, warmed up, the vehicle did fine, even passed a car or two. Rumbling toward their destination, the autumn air swept soothingly through the cab's open windows, toweling Mizzou dry. The squat man liked the breeze too, and neither talked, just sat quietly, staring into the distance at northern California; staring at the skyline of the world's most steep city. "The City," itself. San Francisco, California.

   Catching the eye, the TransAmerica building mesmerized, since both only stared into space, not speaking--nor thinking actually. Focusing upon that building's peak, and city scape backdrop--an iceberg-sea-of-concrete--Mizzou broke silence. "Smythe, you megashrimp. I'm six feet eleven and three-quarters inches. You're what. Maybe five-five on your tiptoes, and you make me bend and stoop going up, then coming down, three flights of stairs to load that royal mental midget?" Smythe released a guffaw. Mizzou cringed, then gritted his teeth. He, too, pulled same stunts on movers unsuspecting the hardship of loading a furniture van in the bay area. Furthermore, to hear Mizzou tell, loading a big-rig within metropolitan San Francisco, with its rolling hills, was tantamount to scaling Yosemite National Park's El Capitan. Whatever, Mizzou was served a double dose of his own medicine, and did not like it. But he learned quickly. The next time that he drove as Van

Captain, the joke would be on Smythe! Next time. "The old bloody, bay shores," Mizzou intoned halfheartedly, and often, "leave a ragged trail of one's blood, sweat, and tears from life's cradle until death and, or, taxes." "Gots to pay your dues, if you wants to sing those blues," Smythe shot back to silence Mizzou. "Cry me a river, Big Guy. My heart, and San Francisco's heart, bleeds for you!"

San Francisco's skyline was Mizzou's favorite topic. He weighed the possibility of buzzing the city's peaks and canyons in a customized ultra light airplane, built to accommodate his gargantuan frame. This might seem impractical, yet in overcoming life's adversity, he proved to be most practical. A transplanted Midwesterner, he came to the west coast in search of his identical twin brother. Seldom were the two united, yet oddly, whenever reunited, much common ground was shared. Even going separate ways, their lives were carbon copies; were monkey-see-monkey-do instant replays. What one did the other had done. For this, their childhood was a gigantic love-hate relationship. Thus, the fissure that split them was forged. But Mizzou was their bloodline. Proud of American Indian ancestry, they were rugged individualists, survivors, and perhaps more pointedly, heirs to oil futures. Their trust fund held millions of dollars in stock. Both knew wanderlust, and both developed fierce independence. Philip was born six minutes before Peter; or was Peter born six minutes before Philip? Whatever, it does not matter except to them. Being first at anything only meant that someone need be second. But the established trust fund did state "that the second born must demonstrate exceptional abilities in life achievement, or forfeit all rights to inheritance." Both Mizzous looked to loophole this technicality by claiming first-born status, and neither really cared who was older. Further, their executor only waved this condition in their faces to motivate them.

"Smythe, the top of the TransAmerica building looks just like a pyramid. I'm telling you, today's date is two thousand BC. Right?" Mizzou channeled gusts of salty ocean air, thick with the fragrance of eucalyptus, into the van's cab, using the window vent like a boat's rudder. He grew excited. His hair flying wildly from the gusting breeze, Mizzou was the joker in a deck of playing cards. He taunted Smythe like he taunted any of his co-workers at Fly By Night Van Lines. In such moods, his expressions were always mischievous. His eyes blazed blue. His coral face magnified, and his left arm, moving forcefully, punctuated every syllable. Rich vocal tones emitted deep from his diaphragm. His phrases rolled from his tongue in waves, just as the ocean rolls to escape the conch. "I'm telling you, Smythe, I've been here before." Smythe politely rolled his eyes upward, but said nothing. "I don't mean here before," Mizzou gestured, "like here in San Francisco, year circa two thousand AD, but I mean here. Like dig it. Wow!

I'm a visitor from time. I come to you from another dimension, that has no limits of time or space. I never was nor never will be. Man, I'm a free spirit!"

"Uh, huh. Free spirit," Smythe sarcastically rebutted, sunburn-pink left arm stuck out the window to promote a breeze through his side of the van, "and I'm Timothy Bleary. Turn on, tune in, drop out! You dig?" Approaching Highway 101, Smythe pulled a stunt that all Fly By Night drivers used. Executed perfectly, it worked. Blasting the van's horn, then stomping on the gas pedal, the van instantly merged with traffic, not needing to slow, not needing to stop. Never mind the confused, terrified, motorists that suffered heart failure--let alone soiled britches--encountering Fly By Night's lumbering land barge. Scapegoating, and adding insult to injury, the drivers and their helpers always screamed and shook fists at their victims. If traffic was light, some drivers still targeted vehicles--just to be mean. Most commonly targeted was the little-old-man, Sunday driver.

Cruising in vintage Rambler, Pacer, Edsel, or some other relic of the past, the little-old-man, wearing straw hat, obediently swerved to prevent a mishap. The van's driver sometimes even extended a middle finger to reinforce this obnoxious act. The little-old-man then waved sheepishly, and boosted his speed to forty-five miles per hour.
Unfortunately, Smythe thought, this time there were no old men to harass.

The truck blazed onto San Francisco Highway

101, its slogan blurred by traffic. Painted in gold lettering against an orange background, upon a brilliant-blue field, the words "Easy Moving" announced that your moving problems were Fly By Night's moving problems. A flapping duck gave this setting motion. Aqua blue, the bird flew through either a rising or setting sun, symbolizing Fly By Night's credo, "No job too big or too small. Arrive by sunup, depart by sunset."

Flowing through traffic, Smythe honked the van horn again and again. "Easy Moving!" he laughed. "Easy Moving! with the Fly By Night birds." "You know, Smythe," Mizzou said, "the people of two thousand BC, the people that built the pyramids, they were the first movers. Don't you think so? I mean they had to be. That's where recorded history starts. Egypt, you know. Am I right? I mean ancient Egyptians labored entire lifetimes, dragging huge stones from quarries so that one kingpin, the boss, the pharaoh, might have a place to crash. Am I right? That's what we do. Right? We spend our entire lives moving objects called furniture from one place to another, so that some schnook has a place to crash. Right? You'd think that in four thousand years, mankind might improve standards. I mean, what the bing, bang, boom. After several millennia, we're still enslaved by a system. That's bad." Smythe and Mizzou always disagreed. Just to be obtuse, if Mizzou said one thing Smythe disagreed, and vice versa.

"I disagree, Philip. Life is a gas. A joke, if you

will. We are born absurd, sure, but we can overcome anything. I mean to say that life isn't to be taken seriously. You know? We should live hard, and live fast, and never look back. Life is a joke and death is the punch line. Yes sir!" Showing that he could dish it out, and take it, Smythe laughed sardonically. "And you're the biggest joke of all!"

Mizzou shot back, "Hardy, har-har. Very funny, Tiny Tim. What do you do for an encore? Sing Tiptoe Through the Tulips?" Smythe scratched his head. "Now that's over my head Big Guy." "Never mind," Mizzou replied, wetting his index finger and drawing an imaginary mark in the air. "Chalk one up for righteousness, 'cause you're too short on brains to understand!" Aside these verbal jousts, Smythe and Philip Mizzou got along.

A benefit of California life that Mizzou greatly appreciated was the weather. The sky was devoid of cloud cover most days and, distantly, snowcapped mountain ranges contrasted the bluest expanse that Mizzou ever beheld--thereby commanding his attention. He daydreamed constantly about what lie just beyond the next hill, or what life might bring tomorrow. Mizzou lived to dream. His other world inspired thoughts that he cared not whether he lived a long life, because he lived his life in stages. He sarcastically told Smythe that coming from another dimension meant that he knew what had happened, ergo, what might happen. He would not say that he manipulated events, only that he anticipated outcome. In his wildest moments, he suggested that he had the power to reincarnate into any period of time and, or, history. He emphasized that the 20th century, because of rapid advancements, ranked best ever--though he did not elaborate.

Perhaps such mental reservation was simple practicality, since Mizzou had no real answers for fellow workers at Fly By Night Van Lines, only wisecracks and cryptic comments. Traffic thickening, Smythe gave the truck's horn another blast. Both started to laugh, and to shout "Easy Moving!" but before their mouths opened, a bright light shuttered an already brilliant afternoon. The flash snapped toward them, blinding both instantly. They were paralyzed. The truck's wheels spun but, hydroplaning, did not move forward. Suspended in space, the van also slumbered in time. Their wrist watches, second hands frozen, read 4:44 p.m.. The light continued pulsing toward them, arcing a brilliant rainbow. Postures erect, eyes transfixed upon the light, a cathexis raced through them that spilled, as a chill, from their chests.

Every color imaginable kaleidoscoped within his head. Without moving, Mizzou was moved. His vision blurred; his senses numbed; his state was euphoric. Placed upon a cold table he maintained same posture but did not move. His clothing fell from his body in folds, dying leaves from a tree. Time flew by, yet seconds seemed eternal. Although disoriented, Mizzou realized Smythe was not beside him--nor did he perceive other life forms. Suddenly he understood! He was not sitting in the truck. He had been transported onto some foreign object. Great googols, this was a spaceship. He was aboard the proverbial UFO.

Further, he was not actually captive upon a table, but floating above it. All about, multicolored beams bathed him amidst a swirl of sensation. The drone of machinery lulled him. Softly, very softly, the mechanized distance attained shape. Voices from the atmosphere became one. His body tingled. He was being probed and that which probed him, the UFO, was mechanized. Though Mizzou could not move, he had no need, for all about, fully 360 degrees, a screen printed data about him. The database was replaced with rapid visualizations that painted his life. Blossoming before him, to include the last move, his existence, expressed as past and present, mirrored upon the screen. Pictured stoop shouldered, Mizzou had finished loading the last piece of furniture from his last move--which was the Katzenjammer job. Adrift within euphoria, Mizzou imagined that he dreamed all this. Computer screen flashed again. Data sprang green and blue. Once again, Mizzou's mind was scanned.

Data-flash: Human. Male Caucasian. Twenty years old. Six feet eleven and three-quarters inches. Height unusual. Considered a giant. Above average intellectual ability. Affluent background. Thinks symbolically.

Data-flash: A free thinker who expresses self

universally. Tendency toward creativity. Borders on emotional brink of confusion and total collapse. Present pathology indicates psychological and physiological problems.

Data-flash: Subject is undernourished and near point of exhaustion but, strong constitutionally. Relies upon intestinal fortitude to endure.

Data-flash: Complete. The screen snow white, Mizzou's mind blanked. His head altered, Mizzou froze in place; a nonentity in time, a nonentity in space.

Chapter 2

Tucked into the most remote corner of Fly By Night's warehouse, a place not even Philibert Sandbar visited, Mizzou carved a hideaway. His comfortable roost boasted every homey amenity. Surrounded by a canyon of storage crates that reached to the roof, his forty-foot square niche was a showpiece. Not restricted by walls, Mizzou strode freely from living room, to bedroom, to dinette set, to kitchenette.

Having wandered into Fly By Night seeking employment, and impressing Sandbar, Mizzou earned appointment to become night watchman. But he did much more than just guard the warehouse and its contents. Needing a roof overhead, Mizzou convinced Sandbar that he could be comfortable, and more efficient, sleeping on the office floor--which perched atop the main entrance of the dilapidated building Fly By Night called home. For appearance sake, Mizzou left his sleeping blanket there, but after a second sleepless night, he uncovered his nesting place.

Randomly, Mizzou had sidetracked the Unger shipment from Zurich, Switzerland, then failed to unload their furnishings into storage crates. Instead, he decorated a spacious cubicle. Unwittingly, the Ungers supplied Mizzou with what he called "cheap copies of Victorian rococo." Mixed within this collection of fragile antiques, Mizzou hung French water colors from the 18th and 19th centuries.

Then one day the telephone rang in Sandbar's office, Sandbar answered, and a very fast talker spoke at the other end. Mrs. Zelman Unger bubbled enthusiastically. "Oh, I do hope my precious furniture arrived unscathed. Ungers were aboard the Mayflower. We know all about moving. I trust that we won't be disappointed." Calling out with megaphone, Sandbar startled Mizzou. "Mizzou! Mizzooou! Philip Mizzou! Front and center!" Booming throughout the warehouse, Sandbar's voice found Mizzou; dirty feet plopped upon Mrs. Unger's favorite rosewood table with mottled grey-on-pink marble top. Aside him sat Big John

Yelverton, a self-styled connoisseur of life's finer things. Looking annoyed, Mizzou blurted, "Great Caesar's ghost, what does Sandbar want now? Damn it!" Big John's eyes flashed. "Time to pay your dues if you're gonna sing the blues, or even think about cheating the piper, big-time."

Faking laughter, Big John hopped to fearfully. Sandbar totally intimidated him. "Go on, Mizzou, see what the blowhard wants so's we can get back to business. I don't want that old buzzard swooping through here uncovering our roost. Go see what he wants." Mizzou's long legs quickly carried him to the other side of the warehouse. Sandbar, cigar in hand, paced nervously, worrying over his telephone conversation with Mrs. Unger

"Now listen, Mizzou," he expelled, pointing spasmodically the moment that the office door opened, "I just got done talking to a very important person. Her name is Zelda Unger. She has money out the mint, so take her stuff from storage and let Yelverton help you load her things onto her truck. She rented one of those do-it-yourself jobbers, and she, with hubby, is arriving anytime."

Mizzou's smile slowly disappeared. With masked emotion he turned 180 degrees, yelped "Right, Fibber, the VIP account! Got it," banged shut the door, and leapt down several squeaky, dusty steps, without his feet once touching tread.

"Do-it-yourself jobs are a pain," he muttered until encountering Yelverton, who, afraid to be caught goldbricking, had moved from the friendly confines of Mizzou's showroom out into the open, and then busied himself folding those furniture pads that went without creases far, far too long.

"What's up, Mizzou?" Yelverton demanded, not stopping his work, afraid that Sandbar might be lurking about. Spying. His paranoia was not unfounded. Sandbar often did just that to keep subordinates under thumb. "Relax, easy money," Mizzou intoned facetiously, "Sandbar didn't tail me. The kid is too smooth. You'll live to scab another paycheck." Laughing, both parked their massive frames onto a crate. Big John's six-six height became less formidable alongside Mizzou. Never at a loss for words, he always enjoyed a joke.

Extending his middle finger, he flashed a grin and said sarcastically, "Here's to you, Mr. Mizzou! I've been scabbing paychecks at this place long before I ever knew freaks like you existed. So here's your IQ, and lunch, all rolled into one, turkey-bird." Not to be outdone, Mizzou responded with, "IQ, my butt. When God disbursed heads, you thought that He said beds, and begged for a soft one."

Before things got too loose, Mizzou updated Yelverton about events. "Yelverton, any minute old-lady Unger is pulling up to that double door and we're under orders to give her the royal treatment." Bemused, Yelverton scratched his head. Cranking a chain that raised a steel door, Mizzou continued. "You see, Yelverton, this lady, I'll call her Lady Unger, owns the furniture that we've parked our carcasses on for so, so long. So now we gots to give it up. You dig? Sandbar says that she has money, friends, pull; so he doesn't want any trouble. We're to be extra, ulta extra and, if we're lucky," he facetiously added, "we're going to get that patented Sandbar incentive bonus."

"What bonus?" Yelverton asked suspiciously. "Why, an all expenses unpaid visit to the unemployment office," Mizzou replied, "so let's do a bang-up job. Huh?" Mizzou winked mischievously at Yelverton, who winked back and said. "Hey, you're talking to the dean, here. The teacher of teachers. Who taught you the business? This Lady Unger is going to get loaded like she's never been loaded. We'll show her what it's like to do business with Fly By Night Van Lines. This one she'll never forget."

Before Mrs. Zelman Unger's furnishings were stacked in a miserable heap near the warehouse loading dock, Sandbar--cigar smoke swirling about him, and ashes flying like sparks from a blast furnace--roared up. "Now listen you camel jockeys, business ain't good and we can't let a type like Zelda Unger bad mouth us. Make sure she gets the real deal. A class-A job. Got that!" "Yeah, right Fibber, don't worry about a thing," Yelverton assured him. "Don't worry about a thing! She's in good hands." Both movers suppressed laughter, but as Sandbar left, Yelverton looked at Mizzou and quizzed sardonically, "Is he serious?" "Sure is," Mizzou replied. "Serious as a heart attack." Both laughed heartily. Then a truck drove up.

A small woman, all business, broke-up their mayhem. Attractive--much unlike the perception that Mizzou had of her--Mrs. Zelman Unger was not some wrinkled relic. Mizzou anticipated someone older than antique furniture, but this little lady was stunning, and easily upstaged the fair maidens present within her French water colors. Mizzou soon realized why her features indeed were all too familiar. Substituting her face for those in the original portraits, some starving artist had ripped-off cheap imitations for a quick buck.

The portrait spoke. "Now hurry, young men. This is a rental truck and time is money. Hubba hubba. Be careful, but my time is not your time." Dock masters were more tactful than this firebrand of a longshoreman, so Mizzou and Yelverton suffered no conscience when, smiling dutifully, they loaded the do-it-yourself van backwards.

"Don't worry, Mizzou," Yelverton whispered, placing Mrs. Unger's rococo love seat atop a very flimsy tier of fragile cartons. "Old lady Unger will get to Paris, or wherever it is she's going, and find matchsticks for furniture. If we run out of pads, we run out of pads." Kicking an unused furniture pad into a corner, he babbled. "All the heavy stuff is on top, see, and with all the shifting and rubbing that happens when a load moves, this stuff will look like kindling for fireplaces.

Surely Mrs. Unger implored them to hurry once too much. Smiling, with the last item crated in a cardboard box, Mizzou ran past her, placed the box at the top of a flimsy stack, and lied, "I meant to compliment you on your decor, mam. We're done, you're loaded, and thanks!" Not tipping them, Zelda Unger climbed into the van's cab, slid alongside her henpecked, silent partner, Zelman--then drove off. Mizzou and Yelverton, holding their breath, finally burst into laughter. This was the dirtiest "trick of tricks" that Yelverton ever taught Mizzou. "The granddaddy of 'em all," he bragged. Distantly, Sandbar's voice boomed, "Mizzooou! Yelverrton! Front and center! The Saxon job is hanging fire!"

Chapter 3

A long and winding street near Telegraph Hill beckoned Mizzou and Yelverton. Popping gears into low, Yelverton mimicked the chug, chug, chugging of ancient Fly By Night van #123. "Come on you lousy gaggle of worthless geese, honk, honk, honk. Crap, or quit!" "Ducks," Mizzou shot back sarcastically, "Ducks. Ducks are not geese, and we are sitting ducks. Ducks go quack, quack, quack in the water, and honk, honk, honk in the sky." Extending his middle finger, Yelverton flashed a grin of white pearls. "One finger for beanie weenie, two fingers for a piece o' my mind. May the gooney bird of Midway Island lay an egg on your beak, you needle-nosed walking encyclopedia. Thanks so much!"

Stopping in front of a rambling gingerbread house, complete with massive stone columns, Fly By Night's finest were met by an energetic man talking a blue streak. "Here comes Mr. Garrulous," Mizzou muttered. "Smile, Yelverton, you know that Sandbar imagines this guy a personal friend." "Ha!" Yelverton snapped, "Sandbar don't know the meaning of the word."

"Well, sir," an affable gentleman beamed, while Mizzou opened the truck's squeaky doors, "mommy and me are excited about this item. It's a precious gift. Well sir, yes sir, yes sirrree. Well sir, take the priceless piano around to the back and through the patio, following the beautiful brickwork, being careful not to scratch it on the thorns from mommy's rose bushes, and then up the steps to that other garden, where you'll find my imported Japanese Zen rock garden and, well sir, yes sir, me and mommy will meet you there, and never mind my imported Japanese gardener, Toy, because, well sir, he doesn't know English, and, well sir, follow mommy's directions because I've prompted her on this: She'll have her arm pointing in the direction that she wants you to go with the thing and, further, well sir, is that understood?"

Grinning from ear to ear, Mizzou and Yelverton followed Mr. Saxon's orders to the letter. After all, they were paid by the hour. "Well sir, I see that you made it this far: Now just follow mommy's arm, that's it, right past the rock garden and straight down this brick walkway until you reach the large French-style doors. Yes sir, well, never mind about the large French doors. Now, sir, keep going. Yes sir, here we are." Mizzou and Yelverton recognized the front of the house. They came full circle.

Oblivious to time and to space, they continued following Mr. Saxon around and around, until they encircled the house once too much. "Mizzou, hour scale or not, I'm burned out and this odd fellow is either putting us on, or he's nutty. Which is it?" "Hey, I need the job, Yelverton. Humor him. Humor him. He's doing a whale of a job. Think of the green, man. Think of the green!"

"Well, sir, now let's see; where is it that mommy wanted her priceless piano?" "Hey lady!" Yelverton blared. "Where do you want the piano?" There was no answer. So following the echo of "Well, sir..." to the rock garden, Mizzou and Yelverton were lost, and could not even depend on Toy for help. He was perched atop a waterfall, comfortable upon a tethered air mattress, sleeping like a log.

"Well, sir, Mizzou, this guy got my goat. Follow me." Reaching the front lawn, Yelverton pushed the heavy cherry-wood piano toward the street. Mizzou's complexion paled; his expression soured; his arms flew toward the sky. "No, Yelverton. No!" Laughing like a mad man, arms flapping in the breeze, Yelverton released his projectile. "Well, sir, priceless piano, good-by, sir, priceless piano."

Rolling slowly at first, the piano gained speed. Saxon, searching frantically for the movers, rushed to the front lawn and did a double take just when the zigzagging roller coaster zipped dangerously past him. Hop-scotching down Telegraph Hill in hot pursuit, Saxon yelped, "Well, well, well sir. My pianoooooo!"

With Cheshire cat grin Yelverton looked at Mizzou, then guffawed. "Damn pianists, they'll do it every time!" Mizzou shook his head with disgust and blurted, "Tell me about it. Too bad about the thingamajig. They're nice people. But all that yak, yak, yak! Man, those yakkety Saxons!"

Comfortable in the van, a fragrant breeze toweled them. Both looked toward the other simultaneously, and with silly faces blurted, "Easy come, easy go, 'Easy Moving!' and all that blow. Give us a call, do what is right, 'Easy Movers' are Fly By Night!"

Chapter 4

For yak, yak, yak and, what is more, for good food and better drink, Sam and Mary O'Blarney's Bar & Grill was the only place in town. Carved into the side of San Francisco's most steep hill, theirs was called by those that loved them--and everyone at Fly By Night adored the couple--O'Blarney's Inn. Put more simply, Fly By Nighters nick-named their favorite home-away-from-home, Sam's. The name Sam O'Blarney suited this rugged individualist. Learning the business from his father, he had tended bar before he could spell it. Barely taller than a bucket, his father let Sam fill up the ice chest now and then. Married by twenty years of age, Sam was a college-of-hard-knocks veteran to his blushing bride. Middle aged, he looked younger than men years his junior. Because he wielded a hardened hickory nightstick, no one dared create a scene in his tranquil little world. That is why Fly By Night movers all respected him, because he never brooked ill will. Always good-natured, and no shrinking violet, he and his bride ribbed Fly By Night's men to pieces.

"Oh, how can I soar with eagles when I'm flying with turkeys," was a favorite, innocuous raspberry that made his patronage sit up and take stock of their situation. Multi talented, Sam was a gifted conversationalist and was never at a loss for words. Fights always took to the streets there. The Fly By Night boys saw to that and, since they were the ones that somehow ended up fighting toe-to-toe close, sassy with booze, and mean for the hell of it, the alleyway behind O'Blarney's Inn made the perfect arena.

The alley's surface was hard to stand on, since the

bricks were slick: mostly from the San Francisco rain; and the San Francisco fog; and the San Francisco bay that crashed blocks away, showering mist throughout immediate neighborhoods. Added to this, the bricks also held a topping of shark oil from those razor-toothed predators that Sam butchered there and, finally; the alley's slope was a killer.

Discarding unused parts of shark into a garbage bin meant stray cats were ever near, picking at the stinking flesh, taming vultures by comparison. A favorite entree devoured by the Fly By Night crew was Sam's pan-fried shark plank, and this morsel became his specialty. With lemon-butter basting, O'Blarney's shark steak was to fight for. "Oh that shark bait, oooh bring theee customer in," he sang again, again, and again. Sam also kept a portable still running full tilt. Secreted away, he dubbed his sure kill snake oil shark juice for its bite. Squat, but all muscle, Sam was tougher than any shark.

He was also the poet laureate of his pub. Written upon the walls of the unisex washroom was an ode to commemorate a spontaneous event at the inn, that occurred whenever Fly By Night's "Easy Movers" were drunk enough, or lucky enough, to bowl a few frames on Sam's alley. Boozers and dead cats were the only ingredients necessary. Factor one element out, and the other element was neutralized. When dead cats, stiff with rigor mortis, littered the alleyway, sober patrons had not the stomach to bowl. When drunk enough, so it went, there were

not dead cats enough. But empty whiskey bottles abounded and made perfect pins. For events of such importance and worldly impact, cat bowling's conditions demanded perfection. With shark oil, rain, and slime to slick his lane, Sam's alley proved ideal to test Fly By Night's keglers' skills.
Recruiting most of its personnel from the streets of San Francisco, Fly By Night's movers were a mixture of drifters, dropouts, dopeheads, and dopes. Sam's commode ode read thus:

It dropped from Sammy's vat that thirsty cat, more dead then drunk, and unable to react. "Scat cat," did one bum chant, but his warning served only as epithet.
"Hey, boys!" he chortled over that very flat cat, "This bowls' in memory for a dearly departed domestic-type cat."
But dipping into same vat all bums did spat, "No wonder, it's rank! So, then, that's that."
"Set 'em up boys," the leaderbum did rant, "The bricks is slick, and excuse me, but I shan't, leave a duckpin upright around this joint here, tonight."
"Tough talk!" the otherbums spat, "Your skill sure is slack." So winding up without any tact, one leaderbum belching breezily, rolled so easily, a gross blob that sleazily, swooped and swarmed a sure-fire hellcat.
Spinning and swirling such a very fast cat, caused the leaderbum to yell, "It's a strike, look at that!" And it smashed the pins forcing most to shatter, but

amidst all of that clatter, the gallery did spatter, "That cat ain't it, just look, not a strike, there shows a split!!!"

Burned out from the Saxon job, Mizzou bellied-up to Sam's bar and, squeezed between Smythe and Yelverton, chided Sam O'Blarney. "Hey bartender, make mine a double, please. Just read the self-styled piece of kaka manure that you term prose." Mizzou minced no words if his mind was frazzled. Sam slung a clear, icy drink Mizzou's way and spat, "Chug-a-lug and choke, Bigfoot." Including his fickle-finger gesture with Mizzou's order, O'Blarney shuffled toward the alley to check conditions for another bowl. Cat bowling was big game, his game, the only game in town.

Mizzou liked Fly By Night's uniform. Khaki, the matching shirt and pants were cool--even fashionable. Wearing a matching pith helmet that he bought from military surplus--full of dust, but otherwise good to go--Mizzou played part-time jungle guide. Drunk, his buddies at O'Blarney's called him the big game hunter. Playing the game, Mizzou called himself a crypto zoologist, not in search of any big game, but exotic big game.

"Typical big game hunters are too mundane," he announced facetiously, quaffing carafe, upon carafe, upon carafe of sparkling Vichy water. This was his drink. H2O with the buzz. No booze, please, for him. "I'm in search of the uncommon: Of the Bigfoot; of the Loch Ness Monster; and of the other assorted dinosaurs, or leviathans of the deep."

"To Bigfoot!" Yelverton burst to his compatriots at the bar. Everyone raised their glasses to toast and to cheer. "To Bigfoot!" all echoed. Barreling in from the alley Sam chimed, "Hey, boys, the bowl's on."

Chapter 5

Mizzou and Big John did not bowl. Never were they drunk enough, or dumb enough, to toss dead animals helter-skelter down some alley. Yelverton preferred to "chase skirt." Mizzou preferred quaffing sparkling water and waxing lyrical about cerebral topics. But one day they blundered into the Club A-Go-Go where nothing at all, let alone skirts, was the native costume. The Club A-Go-Go girls danced au naturel. A favorite go-go dancer was Pandora. Part of her act, one discovered, included a strange pink contraption attached to her derriere. She strutted about the stage more grand than any peacock, au naturel, but for sheer hosiery and a cheap prop. Shaking, rattling, and rolling, pink smoke jetting from the square, her dance was unique. Talent was marginal, but she did a-go-go. All 36-24-36 of her.

"Hey, Pandora," Yelverton heckled, barely inside the door, "strut your stuff. Go for it, baby. Go for it!" Mizzou bubbled with enthusiasm too but, once inside the building, went slack-jawed finding himself at a rare loss for words.

The bouncer gave both a customary warning. Six feet six inches tall, but wider than either Fly By Nighter, Knuckles, the bouncer, grabbed Yelverton and pinned him to the wall. "Whoa, boy. Down, big fella," Big John begged. "We'll be good." Facially deformed, Knuckles mouth puckered. "Make sure of it, huh?" Knuckles cautioned. "Club A-Go-Go don't give no refunds. Huh?" Puckering his mouth in mock protest, Yelverton halfheartedly apologized. "Hey, forgive and forget. Huh?" Mizzou joined in. "Yeah, big fella. This is all just one big misunderstanding. Huh?" Knuckles finally let go and grunted, "Yeah, and let's make sure. Huh? I'll be watching youse both."

Pandora disappeared into a puff of pink haze. Mizzou ordered a sparkling water. Big John--light-headed from the beers he guzzled leaving O'Blarney's in a flash--threw-up all over the bouncer. Knuckles was not happy. He grabbed Big John Yelverton, bounced him rudely across the club's dance floor, and flipped him into the night. Mizzou hurried behind but could not prevent Knuckles picking Yelverton up, then pitching him onto the street. An animated bowling ball, Yelverton hooted pathetically, spewed profanity, then lofted helplessly down another steep San

Francisco hill.

The ugly bouncer moved menacingly toward Mizzou, and reached him just as a size twenty-two, double-wide pontoon caught that fleshy mass square between the eyes. Knuckles dropped more quickly than a lead balloon; more quickly than a dirty-dog-bad-ass, with a lousy dose of diarrhea, dropping hasty britches in the outhouse. One thing that Mizzou did not brook was the bully.

Chapter 6

Mark Twain once wryly said that the coldest winter he ever spent was a summertime in San Francisco. With this in mind, Mizzou and Yelverton might better have known than to do the Wisenheimer move wearing only their khakis. San Francisco days are often temperate, and some say that Indian summer is more temperate than other seasons, but ocean breezes sweeping San Francisco bay chill to the bone. Needless to say, the island called Alcatraz has breezes and temperatures that thicken blood.

As keeper of the lighthouse, Simon Wisenheimer lived quietly and alone, but he telephoned Philibert

Sandbar and requested, "Two strapping young bodies to move me to the mainland." Nothing just ups and leaves Alcatraz, save sea gulls, but Simon Wisenheimer had reason.

After more than fifty years care taking, he was retiring. Wisenheimer was one hundred and one years young. "Yes, sir, I saw them all, sonny. I saw them all." Scratching his thick head of hair, Wisenheimer's deep, blue eyes pierced Mizzou. He continued, "But I never, in all my natural days, laid eyes on the likes of you. How tall are you?" "Six feet eleven and three-quarters inches," Mizzou replied yawning. Wisenheimer squinted and brought his spectacles down from his forehead. "You're taller than, say, you weren't one of them American Indians that took over the island...no, come to think of it, I saw someone just a few months ago...on television...a clown in the circus. He was tall. No, it couldn't be...you never worked for the circus did you?" "No, never-ever," Mizzou blurted sarcastically, packing the last of Wisenheimer's kitchen goods. He expounded for Wisenheimer: "The circus is a ploy to rip-off the consumer by enslaving wildlife. Big game thrives in the wilds, not the circus, and not in zoos either."

Yelverton overheard the conversation and stuck his head into the kitchen long enough to become unwanted. "Don't listen to him, old-timer," he encouraged. "Anyone that doesn't drink his bath water stinks. Don't worry about him, pop, he's just high with the helium of his own thought." "Bath water, indeed," Mizzou rebutted, "I don't use bath water. That's another affront. I bathe nature's way. I take air baths. Bare to the sun, my back to the wind, mother nature caresses me to her bosom with sweet eucalyptus breath, and I love it!"

"Air baths, indeed," Wisenheimer interrupted. "You're both pulling my leg. Everyone knows that the best bath is a steam bath. I turn on the hot water and steam clean in the necessary room. It's the best elixir in the world for health, and prosperity, and long life. Clean living, now that's the ticket. That, and easy living. Never do anything hard. Heck, moving from this island is the hardest thing I'll ever do, and the biggest step I've ever taken, including learning to walk, and I should know 'cause I'm a Czech!"

Curious, then, that Simon Wisenheimer keeled over the minute he set foot upon the mainland. After one hundred and one years of clean, easy living, "Easy Moving" dropped him in his tracks. Mizzou read aloud the note stuffed into Wisenheimer's blue, poplin shirt. "To whom it may concern: I, Simon Wisenheimer, caretaker of Alcatraz, dazzling pearl of the Pacific, do hereby bequeath all my worldly goods to uncle Sam. P.S. Now I lay me down to sleep, a bag of peanuts at my feet, if I die before my mates, give my nuts to roller skates."

"Wise acre!" Yelverton muttered. "Yes, but an old wise acre," Mizzou countered. "Old Wisenheimer, here, walked the walk, and talked the talk. To him it was all so easy. He just didn't realize that you don't walk away from Alcatraz and live to talk about it."

Chapter 7

"Can you believe Sandbar?" Mizzou complained to Yelverton. Gazing at the crumpled work order, damp from the sweat of his khakis, he chided his boss' business sense. "He forgot the address again. And this name. I swear he gets jobs from the telephone book."

Mizzou thumbed through the San Francisco directory until he reached the last page. "Now let's see. Zzyzzx, Zzyzzx, Zzyzzx. Ah, here it is, Yelverton, the last name in the damn book. I swear. With a name like Zzyzzx...sounds like a crypto zoological name to me." Whenever Mizzou used technical language, Yelverton responded with big words of his own. "Mizzou, you discombobulated boob, I don't care if you name your favorite social disease Zzyzzx, long as you pay your dues. All the Zzyzzxs need are greenback dollars and they're golden. Now get them on the horn and let's make a buck.

"Hey, man, out of sight. Yeah, man, that's right,

Haight and Ashbury. We're in the upstairs flat. Yeah, man, the only upstairs flat. Yeah, is the piano alright, man? I mean, dig, your outfit told you that we live at the top of the building. Right?" "Talk about your damn lousy luck, Mizzou bitterly complained to Yelverton. This piano goes to the top of the apartment. I'll bet you that it's winding stairs, and at least six flights. Oh, my aching sacroiliac!"

"Yeah, another lousy piano job," Yelverton sighed, "but let's give it a tickle just the same." His mood soured and he grabbed his back in mock protest. "Leave it to Sandbar to bid on these jobs."

The upright piano was the biggest, ugliest thing that Mizzou ever moved. Pink, with purple polka dots, he thought it the sick result of artistic humor. "What a joke!" he complained, rolling the piano onto the sidewalk. "Yelverton, we'll never make it. Call Sandbar and demand more help. We're screwed!" "There are no more helpers," Yelverton replied. "You forget that Sandbar filed Chapter Eleven bankruptcy last week. We need these jobs so that he can hire more men.

"Hey, man," the young man with a golden tan said, "over here." Sticking his greased head out a distant window, hairstyle scarf flapping in the breeze, he could not be missed by the pair. "Who's that?" Yelverton queried. "There, atop Mount Buttbuster." Pointing toward the sky, Mizzou whined, "Our assignment." "Oh, my aching hemorrhoids!" Yelverton fumed.

A woman appeared at the building's entrance. Fat, with oily red hair growing from an oiler red scarf, she was the fattest, ugliest creature that Mizzou ever met. "Where do you want the piano, lady?" he asked facetiously. She replied matter of factly. "Straight up. Six flights."

After most of the morning, and only three flights navigated, Mizzou and Yelverton realized that, maybe, if neither died, the summit might be mounted. Say in a week or so.

"Hey, man, come on, you're dogging it!" Zzyzzx implored once too often. "Now, movers, be very careful not to scratch my beautiful pink finish," the other Zzyzzx scolded. Neither one should so much as opened their mouth, let alone dare to speak. Frustrated trying to free the piano from a jam on a very tight turn, Mizzou and Yelverton merely looked at one another, threw their arms into the air, and "walked the walk."

"Hey, you fools!" Zzyzzx admonished. "Get back here and free my piano!" "A damn dirty plot!" Mizzou spat hoarsely. "There ought to be laws against pink pianos." Yelverton mixed his words with contempt. Spitting venom deadlier than a rattler's, he shook and hissed, "That's what one gets when one schmooses with a cross between a moose and a mouse. Leave it to Sandbar to amuse himself by sicking the ne'er-do-well dregs of society on us."

Chapter 8

Perhaps Yelverton influenced Mizzou badly.
Perhaps Mizzou badly influenced Yelverton.
Whether Chapter 11 bankruptcy demoralized them,
or low morale forced filing Chapter 11 does not
matter, for every job that Mizzou and Yelverton
undertook was shrouded in doom before they even
set foot upon any household's threshold.

The Queasy homestead proved no different
within their world of farce. All that needed doing
was to simply pack the Queasy furnishings into
heavy-duty, cardboard boxes, load them--along with
heavy furniture, appliances, and so forth--into seven
foot square crates, and to then send the whole kit
and caboodle to Zurich, Switzerland. "Why Zurich,
I'll never know Mizzou," Yelverton queried,
scratching his backside. "Everything going to
Europe must pass through Zurich first," Mizzou
hypothesized, "because it's Europe's way of keeping
the continent concentric. No, it's really a plot," he
concluded. "Furthermore, Europe chose
Switzerland because it affords everyone the
opportunity to convene and to vote on new arrivals.
You know, like a steering committee, or, better yet,
a welcoming committee. It's all so convenient. If
they don't like you, they just shuttle you through a

clearinghouse and, slam-bang, get your can out of my corner of the world." Yelverton laughed. "I don't give a crap what they do. Farthest I've ever been away from the streets of San Francisco was Sausalito, and that was just to see the skyline all lit up. Gees, it's so beautiful at night. Just like a Christmas tree. You know, Mizzou, now that's the world's most beautiful view.

Mizzou wiped his brow with the fire engine-red bandana that he kept handy for tidying, should he need to present a more respectable image to Fly By Night's "better clientele," whose favor Sandbar curried. He worked a brass door knocker with abrupt, distinct, piercing precision at the doorstep of a very impressive Victorian mansion, that survived in testament to an ilk of seafarers who frequented gambling houses and brothels in a district once called the Barbary Coast.

Suddenly the door swung open, and a sour-faced-red-bearded basketball of a man stood, hands full of fudge cake, looking with condescension at some working-class stiff. "What kind of ecosystem reject has Philibert Sandbar uncovered this time?" he oozed between gobs of frosting mush that agitated within his mouth. Meaning Mizzou's pith helmet he unabashedly suggested, "What's that atop your noggin, a bucket?"

Standing six-six and weighing three hundred plus pounds, Excelsior Xavier Queasy did not look the part of psychiatrist, if indeed there be a mold into which that group must fit. But Mizzou's environment dealt often with the unusual or the absurd, so behavioral scrutiny by this gargantuan specimen of dysfunction did not bother him. He cared not what Dr. E. X. Queasy thought anyway. If Mizzou disliked someone, he labeled that person as loosey-goosey and bashed away. "Daffy ducks don't quack at me!" he joked to Yelverton, "I'm bad!"

"Oh, yeah, Mizzou, you're bad!" Yelverton egged-on. "But I'll tell you what's really bad," he enthused, almost unable to contain excitement. "I was in the garage getting some wedges to stick under one twenty-three's wheels. And, wow! You ought to get a gander at the exotic roadster parked there. I know automobiles like the back of my hand, but, this baby--just can't figure what Dr. Turkeybird is doing with a treasure like that!"

Humongous rolls of fat folded upon Queasy's body, and he moved like the great, white whale that he was. Gorging upon more double-fudge and double-thick brownies, his face undertook the color of dirt. Mizzou called him "the great mudpie." "Exquisite nickname for that odd-duck," Yelverton chortled--before labeling Queasy, "That grand blimp from Cloud Nine, high by the helium of his own thought."

Overhearing them, Queasy was enraged. "Now see here," he steamed. "Get your bossman. I'll not be addressed by anyone with that tone of voice." "Now you've gone and done it," Mizzou cautioned. "Sandbar won't like this one bit." "Oh, I'm sweating bullets Big Guy," Yelverton blabbed. Fly By Night Van Lines ain't your basic top ten, New York Stock Exchange wise. Matter of fact, they ain't your basic top ten moving company. Thinking about it, they ain't top ten nothin'. They're minus ten, and I don't give a gust in September's wind anyway."

Before Mizzou and Yelverton even finished licking the platter of double-fudge brownies that Queasy left on a shaded patio, Sandbar, arms spinning like the paddles of a windmill, swooped in--a buzzard anticipating the kill. He admonished Mizzou, then threatened Yelverton. How he happened in so suddenly, only he and Queasy knew.

"I warned you Yelverton," he hissed, "this is the last straw. You'll be fired the next time something like this happens. Believe me, there is no place in my organization for a goof-off. Got that?" Sandbar looked from the corner of his eye to see if Queasy bought his act. The doctor did, for his hostile posture relaxed. Once again he munched on goodies, and took from his pocket the biggest candy bar that Mizzou ever saw. It was the king-sized kind that stores sell for families to share as desert. But in Queasy's fat hands, the bar was a mere appetizer.

Suddenly, and without further provocation, Sandbar blared, "On second thought Yelverton, you're fired." "Why?" the big guy retaliated. "Because one, you're lazy; two, you're getting lazier; and three, you're giving me indigestion." Sandbar belched greatly, causing sparks, cinders, and ashes to fly into the air from his ever-present cigar. His expression soured and he pounded his closed fist upon his chest. "You can't fire me, I quit!" Yelverton fired back. Mizzou butted into the conversation, "Don't forget unemployment Big Guy. If you quit, you don't draw it." "On second thought," Yelverton drawled, "I accept your offer Sandbar."

Abruptly, then, Yelverton's lackluster career with Fly By Night Van Lines ended. "Mizzou, sit tight," Sandbar ordered, "I'm sending Smythe over. You're to help him with the Katzenjammer account." Mizzou scoffed, "Account, indeed." Lest clients overhear the real deal, Sandbar always called jobs, accounts.

Yelverton disappeared onto a boulevard, and Sandbar gave him the traditional "Easy Mover" farewell. "There goes another bird in the breeze," he chortled, flipping Big John his middle finger. "Don't let the door hit you on the butt when you leave!"

Chapter 9

By most standards, Smythe was short. Only

five-five, he looked comical standing alongside Mizzou at six eleven and three-quarters inches. But if Smythe looked comical, then Katzenjammer looked hilarious alongside the Big Guy (this redwood of people), because Katzenjammer made Smythe look tall.

He waddled from a spotless apartment in an immaculate apartment house, ready smile parting his friendly face, and surprised the stars out of the "Easy Movers." Because of size, Homer Herman Katzenjammer always had work with sideshows, circuses, and other various, sundry sidelines. Only thirty-nine inches tall, Katzenjammer billed himself the "smallest man in the world."

Smythe took charge after inventorying Katzenjammer's residence. "Mizzou, you tend the truck and I'll be along. Make sure all of the pads are clean, and sweep the floor." "Yes, master," Mizzou grinned, saluting Smythe. "Right away, Van Captain, sir." Snapping to, then stooping through the doorjamb, he exited the apartment. "Good help is so hard to find," Smythe apologized to Katzenjammer, "but why leave a nice place like this?" "Well, the little lady passed, and I'm just knocking about in this big ol' place with nothing to do all day but stare at four walls. Just remember, no man is an island, nor a rock. I'm moving more uptown, nearer the excitement, into a smaller, comfier abode. I found a little walk-up in the Haight-Ashbury district and that is what I need. I'm too depressed living here alone. I want to live."

"Yeah, right, live," Smythe agreed, rolling his eyes and wrinkling his eyebrows, "life is too short."

Cackling, he grabbed Katzenjammer's overstuffed easy chair, expelled a breathy grunt, mumbled "I gotcha," then maneuvered down the sidewalk with the sure-footed step of a mountain goat. After placing the piece on the van, Smythe busied himself folding pads. From that point forward, Mizzou did all the loading. Smythe was typical of Fly By Night movers. He pulled rank constantly, goldbricked with the best of men, and let the new kid on the block do all the dirty work.

"Are you sure that I haven't seen you some place before?" Katzenjammer queried Mizzou, scratching his bald pate. "I never forget a face, and yours is very familiar." "Sorry to disappoint, old-timer, but I sure as shooting wouldn't forget, and I've never, ever seen you before--of that, I am positive." "Oh, well, but you're certain you've never been to Las Vegas? You know, Circus Circus."

"Great googols, Smythe! That Katzenjammer guy is driving me crackers with all those questions. Let's load and get the Sam Hill gone." Smythe concurred, "One more trip and we're good to go. After you." Smythe pointed toward the apartment house. Job done--perhaps their last--Smythe and Mizzou drove away.

Chapter 10

A cathexis raced through Mizzou that spilled, as a chill, from his chest. His head spun. Colors exploded like fireworks before his eyes. A rainbow arched the sky, painted the windshield brilliantly, and affected his vision's focus. Gradually, though, his sight returned. Shaking his head, he exclaimed, "Man, what a buzz! What was that, Smythe?" "Say, what are you talking about?" Smythe returned. "You know, the light, the voices, the psychic energy field."

"Man," Smythe chided, "you have been acting strangely since the Queasy job. You been eating dog food?" "Yeah, that's it!" Mizzou exclaimed. "That blimp Queasy laced his brownies with hallucinogens. I must have gone on a trip. I think. More likely, though, my subconscious mind played tricks with me. I'm into astronomy, my brother, Peter, is into astrology; therefore, I fantasized visiting a flying saucer!" His argument was mostly false bravado.

"You were on a trip alright," Smythe agreed. "Say, let's call Sandbar and tell him we'll unload Katzenjammer some other time. You're in no shape!" "Fine with me Smythe. Say, let's pop in to Sam's saloon and sop-up some liquid refreshment. I need it!" "Yeah, I need a beer to boot," the squat man agreed, scratching his dry throat. You buy, huh?"

Quaffing their drinks--sparkling water for

Mizzou, and Anchor Steam for Smythe--made them looser than old boots, and both waxed lyrical about "Easy Moving." "You know the damnedest thing about moving?" Mizzou confessed. "Getting started!" "Yeah," Smythe agreed, "getting started, like one of Fly By Night's vans, say old one twenty-three, is nearly impossible."

Mizzou, suffering a light-headed funk from Queasy's brownies, rambled. "Have you been reading about the latest space probes Smythe?" Smythe lied, "Sure, you mean Pioneer or Explorer, right?" "Wrong!" Mizzou shot back, pointing his index finger skyward. "Those were light years ago. I mean the Voyager missions Van Captain dunce. Do you realize that eventually either of these craft might accomplish what no other man-made object has accomplished. Think of it! These craft will leave our solar system and travel into the void of space forever. Eternity! Now that's what I call 'Easy Moving.' Do you realize the implications? What if either makes contact. You know, with intelligent beings."

Smythe blew his cool. "One, there is no extraterrestrial life in space; two, we'd best keep our own priorities in line here at Fly By Night, without agonizing over spaceships; and three, I don't approve of the naked people on the Voyager things, because if God had intended for man to roam naked, He wouldn't have expelled Adam or Eve from the garden of Eden. Now would He?"

Mizzou laughed but, puzzled, merely deferred

and said, "Right you are, Smythe. Right you are." He gazed out the sparkling picture window toward California's blue sky.

Someone overheard their conversation and introduced himself. "I'm Thornberry Newberry Teaberry, TNT for short, and believe me young man, you know of what you speak...why, the implications of the vastness of the universe, the mere theory of the Big Bang, quasars, novas and supernovas, black holes, neutron stars, et al...just boggles the mind. Realizing the minutia of our microcosm, versus the infinitude of the stellar phenomena...well, anything is possible--we just are not wise enough to admit that we don't know what we don't know.

Hoping that after one hour of non-stop babble Teaberry's knowledge of astronomy might be exhausted, Smythe was dismayed that TNT merely shifted gears, then launched discourse to include astrophysics. The bar's clock read 4:44 a.m.. "Saved by the bell," Smythe whispered when Sam announced, "Drink 'em up, boys--last call!"

Darkness enveloped the town--Thornberry Newberry Teaberry called it "the edge of dawn"--and down the hatch with their final-final drinks, all left O'Blarney's. Streaming down the open road, Fly By Night Van Line's #123, headlights blazing, tore upon night's black mantle. Traffic flowed smoothly, pouring forth a time-exposed stream of yellow light. A sleek, exotic roadster passed through the path of the truck's headlights, glowing golden and orange.

Smythe, woozy from too many brews, steered cautiously. He lit and slowly puffed upon another cigar, letting the ashes scatter crazy quilt onto the highway. "Smythe," Mizzou blurted, "stop the truck. I'm sick!" He threw-up his guts. Finished, the color returning slowly to his cheeks, he told Smythe, "You go back to the warehouse without me. I'm in no shape to face Sandbar. He'll leave the warehouse keys in that secret niche, and I'll get them later. Alright?" "Right, you got it."

Smythe revved the truck's engine, popped the gears into low, and headed downtown. "Man, the city lights are outstanding," Mizzou whispered, his breath escaping into crystal clouds against the icy autumn air. "Yelverton's right, this town is the world's showpiece. A diamond is a diamond, yet a diamond doesn't sparkle more grandly than these brilliant beacons."

Wrapping the khaki shirt like a scarf about his neck, Mizzou stole a last glance at Fly By Night van #123. Vanishing slowly into bulbous clouds of noxious fumes, Smythe steered the ancient vehicle into a fallen onyx backdrop, which mirrored the pulsing, cosmic lighting of northern San Francisco. "That could be Voyager, streaking toward the outer limits," Mizzou intoned softly. Then with hesitation he turned, and moved silently into the night.

Chapter 11

Days passed before the bankruptcy courts ruled
that Fly By Night's assets would be auctioned off
and the monies distributed to outstanding creditors.
Big John Yelverton had not found gainful
employment nor, for that matter, had Philip Mizzou.
Both did find that misery loves company, though,
and so, sitting over cool drinks at O'Blarney's Inn,
drinking beer and Vichy water, both puzzled about a
course of action.

"You know, Mizzou," Big John mused, clinking
an empty beer bottle against the full one that Sam
O'Blarney set down, "what we need is a sure-fire
scheme to make some bucks. I have a little set
aside--money that is. How about you?" "You know
me, Big Guy," Mizzou sighed, not knowing what
was buzzing through John Yelverton's mind, "I have
enough squirreled away for a rainy day."
Yelverton's tone grew sarcastic as he blurted, "Oh,
piss on my shoe, a rainy day. From what I hear you
could buy and sell Sandbar, or Fly By Night Van
Lines, if you really wanted to. I have this great idea,
my man. Let's you and me pool our cash and buy
the straight truck--you know, one twenty-three. If
we're lucky, we'll get it for a song and dance. A few

thousand, tops. The bucket of bolts don't look like much, and not too many will bid on it. With what I know about mechanics, I'll fix it up, and then you and me will go into business for ourselves, you know, moving furniture."

Mizzou laughed hard. Slamming his drink upon the bar he exclaimed, "And just what do we do for customers, and what do we call ourselves, and what about charging for our services?" "Easy!" Yelverton shot back. "We won't use the Fly By Night name because that's taken but, listen, I have given a lot of thought to a name--a lot of thought." "So, enlighten me, take me out of suspense. What's the name, Yelverton?" Big John Yelverton's chest swelled with pride. He presented best posture to sit erect upon the bar stool, and with a mischievous grin said, "The name of our business will be...For The Birds Trucking."

Mizzou nearly choked upon a mighty gulp of sparkling water. Spitting his drink amidst uncontrollable laughter, he sprayed Yelverton and blurted, "That is absolutely the dumbest name I have ever heard for a business! But what the bing, bang, boom. What's in a name? People buy price not fancy labels. So what do we charge for the jobs?" Yelverton wiped his face dry with his red bandana and replied, "Easy. Each move is billed by the hour for two men and the truck. So we'll have to hustle to keep customers happy. I figure maybe seventy-five or eighty dollars an hour. And don't forget, we're on the clock from the warehouse, and we get riding time from residence to residence. We can't loose, Mizzou!"

Ever pragmatic, Mizzou rebutted. "What about insurance? What about a thousand other incidentals that Sandbar could not deal with?" "Ah Mizzou, come on, now, you're hedging. We'll buy the straight truck, paint over the old name with our new name, and give it our best shot. Just think, my man! We'll be our own bosses. We'll call our own shots! You're either with me or you're not! Are you with me?" Mizzou finished his drink, looked Yelverton straight in the eye, and said firmly, "Yeah."

Chapter 12

Philibert Sandbar was a nervous wreck at the public auction. If lucky, his lowly assets would barely cover his liabilities. By settling for fifty cents on the dollar, most creditors walked away thinking that something was always better than nothing. Yelverton and Mizzou thought so too, but neither was a fan of Sandbar, especially in light of the shabby treatment that Yelverton received with his firing; so neither felt sorry for the pathetic figure twitching at the eye and belching bad gas caused by a peptic ulcer, further aggravated by bad cigars.

Sandbar proved oblivious to his surroundings, focusing his attention on the auctioneer. Scribbling every dollar amount for every item sold into his notebook, Sandbar kept a running sub total, gulping fearfully with each new addition, and cringing spasmodically all the while, as if the skies might open and a grand piano come smashing down upon him should he not foot a proper bottom line.

Yelverton relished every expression of surprise, every fearful grimace upon Sandbar's face. "Just look at old buttbreath now, Mizzou. He who laughs last, laughs best I always say. Hey Mr. Buttbreath! Got a match?" Yelverton chided. Big Guy answered himself to the delight of some. "Yeah, your face and my butt."

Mizzou, speaking over laughter, broke in. "Shut up, big mouth, the straight truck will be auctioned next. You did bring your share of the cash?" "You bet, Mizzou. I have my twenty-two hundred if you have yours. And don't forget. I've been to plenty of these horse-trading shows, so I'll do all the signaling. We'll get old one twenty-three for thirty-three hundred tops, and with what's left over, we'll fix it up. So don't get excited."

Sandbar was oblivious to everything but the auctioneer and dollar amounts that he scribbled for subtotals on his scratchpad. The auctioneer wielded his wooden mallet like a mighty hammer, pounding it with a barked-out sollld, after each sale. Describing Fly By Night straight truck #123 as "A reliable utility vehicle with great fixer-upper potential," he drew hearty laughter from the gallery when the vehicle backfired and failed to start. The bidding started at nine hundred dollars.

"Ladies and gentlemen, I present to you a genuine article of yesteryear; when the internal combustion engine used regular gasoline instead of unleaded; before our sunny and golden coast was polluted by the noxious fumes of too many vehicles. Before...," the auctioneer was cut to the quick. "Ah, shut up with the phony baloney and get to the sale. That bucket of bolts is a diesel-powered plant anyway--not gasoline. Quit blowing it out your exhaust pipe and let's bid. Now!"

Yelverton was in rarest form. Giggling women and children turned to express their approval. No nonsense working men, tanned from a long, hot summer spent laboring under a sweltering sun, joined in. "I'll bid nine-fifty," one man cried. "Make that one thousand even," another bid countered. "Ten hundred and fifty," Yelverton blurted enthusiastically, winking at Mizzou, then poking him in the ribs. "This will separate the men from the boys, good buddy. From here on out things will get fast and furious and then drop like a dead duck. So pay attention to the program," Yelverton chortled. "You're learning from the master!"

Chomping on a trademark, foul-smelling cigar, Sandbar was no less nervous with the auction of #123 than any other item at his warehouse. But this old workhorse of a truck did have sentimental value, as it was the first vehicle in a long line of vans not

to come and go at Fly By Night. He brushed aside a
shimmering droplet from his face, that certainly was
a tear not sweat, and continued fidgeting with his
pencil, wanting to jot down the last few dollar
amounts and be done with the ordeal of his
bankruptcy. No fool at life, Sandbar had squirreled
away thousands in a secret Swiss bank account. He
was flying out of San Francisco that night, "to
vacation and arrange for retirement."

"Ten hundred and fifty, ten hundred and fifty. Do
I have eleven, eleven...?" the auctioneer sang,
pointing his wooden mallet in the direction of the
bidder. "Do I have eleven-fifty? Eleven-fifty?
Eleven-fifty?"

Yelverton raised a bulky arm high into the air, but
before the auctioneer called his bid, he sang,
"Thirteen hundred! I have thirteen hundred from
the man in the Caterpillar hat. Do I have fourteen
hundred, fourteen hundred. Do I...?"

Yelverton raised his arm high again, with all five
fingers flashing and flexing like a gaggle of flying
geese. "Fifteen hundred. I have fifteen hundred
from the man with the tall friend. Do I have...?
Seventeen hundred bid by the man in the Cat hat.
Seventeen hundred is the bid."

Bidding volleyed furiously, bouncing about the
crowd, then back and forth between Yelverton and
the Caterpillar hat, until reaching thirty-three
hundred dollars and, as expected, Yelverton
presented that bid, then waited with baited breath
when the auctioneer chimed, "I have thirty-three

hundred. I have thirty-three hundred. Do I have thirty-four? Thirty-three hundred once, thirty-three hundred twice, sollld, to the big man with the little pork-pie hat for thirty-three hundred dollars."

"Whoooboy! California, here I come!" Yelverton exclaimed, jabbing Mizzou in the rib cage. "Get your money ready, my man. For The Birds Truck Lines just sprang wings and is blowing this chicken coop!"

Chapter 13

Yelverton wasted no time overhauling and re-painting old #123. "You know, Mizzou, you won't regret this investment. Believe me good buddy, wait until you see the money we'll make. Huh? What am I saying?" Big John puzzled, scratching his backside, then reaching for a very greasy monkey-wrench.

Clanging the tool against the muffler, he cussed bitterly and coughed spasmodically, choking against exhaust soot backed up in the pipes. "I forgot that you are richer than Wells Fargo," Big John mused sarcastically. "What do they call it? Nouveau Riche? How's that for big words, Mizzou? Bet you thought that I didn't have it in me...big words."

Mizzou laughed--because Yelverton's face turned gray from engine soot--but managed to rebut. "That money is tied up in trust for another year or so, but doesn't matter, 'cause I'm an entrepreneur deluxe, and my money is on the line. Remember whose blood, sweat, and tears helped finance this operation, big man. Were in this together. Win lose or draw. You know, another benefit of the freewheeling lifestyle that comes with the territory will be the wanderlust factor," he added, arms folded confidently across his chest while he rocked upon his heels, watching Yelverton work.

"What's this, this wanderlust factor?" Yelverton puzzled--curiosity aroused. "You know," Mizzou countered, "a bonus of being your own boss. When the opportunity arises to take off and see the countryside, finding more work, or just looking for adventure, you just go. You know, just do it! The only thing keeping us tied down is our own lack of inspiration. And further, we'll be earning an honest buck."

"What do you mean by that?" Yelverton queried. "Remember that time at the Queasy job, and Sandbar came by and got on our cases? Well, you know that we both freaked out on those crappy brownies that fatso put out, but more to the point, when Sandbar showed up, I saw him talking to Queasy in his study while I pretended to pack some books. I overheard Sandbar and Queasy, and guess what?"

"Mizzou," Yelverton replied testily, "I hate guessing games. What!" "Well, I can't prove this, Big Guy, but I saw Sandbar hand a package to Queasy, and then Queasy gave Sandbar cash money. You see what I'm getting at now?" Yelverton was totally confused, but pretended to know. Raising an eyebrow he said, "Uh, huh."

"I suspect that Sandbar was dealing drugs on the side, Yelverton! We were working for a dealer and didn't know it. Sandbar used Fly By Night Van Lines as a front for drugs. It was the perfect cover. Any shipments coming from out of state, or out of country for that matter, carried drugs! Yelverton, we were all used! That's why Sandbar didn't keep movers around long. That's why he fired you for no real reason. He would have fired me too, but only needed me until the auction. No big deal." "That son-of-a-gun," Yelverton sighed, "I didn't think that simpleton had the gumption for something like that." "Well, whatever, Big Guy," Mizzou cautioned. "You can bet that we've seen the last of Sandbar. He'll bury his head in the sand along the Mediterranean and never surface. That's behind us. We're in charge now, and we'll deal with one another straight and narrow. Deal?" Mizzou extended his large hand to grasp another large hand. "Deal," Yelverton affirmed. "You take care of the Xs and the Os, my man, I'll take care of the truck. We ignore the funny little pills for sure, and we'll let wanderlust take care of itself."

"About the wanderlust thing," Mizzou added, you

know that some jobs will take us to the far corners of California's borders--maybe beyond borders if we want that kind of work. We ought to be prepared to seek adventure and maximize our opportunities. You know, Yelverton, turn every-day routine into a holiday. For instance, if we get over to the Sierra Nevadas, we would be foolish not to do some hiking along the redwood trails, and I wouldn't mind visiting Yosemite National Park to see El Capitan. Maybe even camp out underneath the stars at night and breath the pure mountain air. You know what else?" Mizzou facetiously offered. "No, tell me. What else?" Yelverton mocked impatiently, wrestling awkwardly with the truck's new muffler. "Bigfoot!" Mizzou responded proudly. "What feet?" Yelverton frowned again, his face turned charcoal from too much exhaust soot.

"You know, Big Guy! The legend of the Northwest Indians--the Sasquatch. Half-man, half-creature. Some of those big boys grow to twelve feet in height and weigh close to a ton." "Ah, go on, Mizzou!" Yelverton barked, banging the muffler into a fitting with a rubber mallet. "Those things are old wives' tales--and further north anyway. They're only spotted in Washington and British Columbia, not California!"

"That's where you're dead wrong," Mizzou rebutted. "There are documented Bigfoot sightings in northern California, too, and most recently, activity has been reported about Yosemite National Park." "Well, what the hell are we supposed to do with one of those things if we spot it, let alone catch it, Mr. Crypto Zoologist? Eat it!" This sarcasm brought more laughter from Mizzou. "No, I dare say that those creatures are too shy and cunning to be seen often, let alone trapped. I'm just talking about enjoying ourselves during the chase. You know, the thrill of the hunt. We keep our priorities, of course. But let's be prepared to grab the good times when we can. Life is too short!" "Uh, huh, you remind me of someone, Mizzou. Smythe used to blow gas out his tailpipe while the other guy did all the work, too. Say, hand me that U-clamp and help with this exhaust system, before I muzzle your mouth with this muffler!"

Chapter 14

Philibert Sandbar paced nervously with his one-way airline ticket to Zurich, Switzerland clutched tightly in a sweaty palm. Puffing upon an ever-present cigar, he ignored the loud-speaker warning that boarding passengers were in a no-smoking area. Oblivious to the admonishments and dirty looks that might kill if legal, he was startled by two burly airport-authority police officers that suddenly appeared to scold and threaten.

"Ok, Mac," one of them patronizingly cautioned, arms folded across his chest, rocking upon his heels, looking almost to topple from this sway. "Let's be a good-fly guy, and go to our seat without the little stinkers that everyone hates so much." Sandbar looked flabbergasted. He was accustomed to barking out orders and pushing others--not being pushed. He tried unsuccessfully to challenge authority. "Now you listen to me...!" he belched, before provoking the second officer to bark. "No, you listen Charlie Brown!" the officer cautioned, pointing to several bright, red-on-white NO SMOKING SIGNS placed about the waiting room. "This is a smoke-free zone, and passengers' lungs, mine too for that matter, are entitled to clean air. You're a one-man-pollution plant...an environmental disaster waiting to happen. San Franciscans breath enough of the smog and dirty crap that floats up the coast from Los Angeles without your exhaust adding to the bilge!"

Without further incident, Sandbar handed over the few cigars that were loose in his sport jacket breast pocket. He even offered an unopened package of five cigars tucked comfortably into a shirt pocket. In further gesture of goodwill, Philibert Sandbar opened his briefcase to produce a full box of Golden Wand special exports, smuggled by the black market via Mexico from Havana, Cuba. What Sandbar did not produce were four other boxes that he had stashed into a carry-on suitcase.

"Never give up your ace in the hole," he mumbled to himself, handing over the box of Golden Wands. "Say what, pal?" cop arrogantly blabbed. "Who's calling whom a lonely loser?" "No, no. You misunderstood me," Sandbar replied defensively. "I was just saying that you have the whole bunch and, you're lucky because these are the best cigars that money can buy." "Just you let us be the judge of that buddy boy!" the arrogant cop snapped, tucking the cigars under his arm before doing an about face.

Walking toward his partner he shared the bounty. Both unwrapped a Golden Wand, and beyond the jurisdiction of the red-on-white NO SMOKING signs, each lit up the finest cigars that money could buy. Smiling with Cheshire-cat grins, they left the no-smoking zone to Philibert Sandbar. Determined not to be upstaged at this juncture by obnoxious coppers, Sandbar popped several breath mints into his mouth; parked his nervous body onto a rigid vinyl and chrome lounge chair; then took several swigs from a small, silver flask that contained a favorite coffee liqueur.

He swallowed the mints whole but did not care. They helped to settle his churning belly. His flight left within the hour. He hadn't realized how exhausted he was. Shutting his eyes, Sandbar fell asleep. Desperate for rest, he snored uncontrollably for a long time.

Chapter 15

Thornberry Newberry Teaberry finished his cup of coffee while asking Sam O'Blarney about the saloon, its history, and the kind of people Fly By Nighters were. "I really can't say enough good things about the men from the furniture warehouse, my friend," O'Blarney replied. "There's not a man there that at one time or another didn't rub me the wrong way and vice versa, but that's business, you know. Even the new boy, you know, the tall kid, Mizzou...as different as he is...heck, I've been in this business twice as long as he is old. He uses all those big words, but he's a good kid, and the men from the warehouse all told me he's a good worker to boot. Tell you what. Now that Fly By Night has closed its doors, I'm going to offer him a job and future with me, here at this tavern. If he takes it, fine. If not, fine too. Mary and me will get along. I'll tell you what, though. I'll miss those fellows from Fly By Night Van Lines. Not that they kept me in business, because they didn't. Most of them owe me money for food and drinks. But the friendships that were formed here over the years are priceless. I'll miss them." Finished washing a stack of beer mugs, Sam O'Blarney lined the glassware in a neat row to dry, and concluded with uncharacteristic, misty eyes. "And I sure hope that they'll miss me."

Teaberry was genuinely touched by O'Blarney's honesty. "I wish that I could say the same thing about my previous employ. Oh, I'm not complaining so much as just expressing disappointment. No, more like disillusionment. You see, I worked for nearly thirty years at the California State Observatory as an astronomer, and while I never expected to head the department, I always felt overlooked by younger, brighter personnel. I'll tell you. Those eggheads that graduated with summa-cum-laude credentials may have had an edge on me scholastically, but there is nothing wrong with me saying that while they could chart celestial navigation perfectly, maybe even prove that E equals MC squared, none of them could go out for coffee, much less find their way back."

Taking a sip of steaming coffee that O'Blarney poured from a freshly brewed pot, Thornberry Newberry Teaberry continued. "I see why you are so moved by the spirit of Fly By Night movers. They are a very colorful bunch, and certainly represent a cross section of San Francisco's population. Maybe I was out of touch with the mainstream too much while gazing at the stars from the observatory. Charting celestial bodies is very rewarding, but also very humbling. I don't know, but maybe I developed some kind of complex working there. You know that the stellar phenomenon is such that throughout man's attempt to measure time, the heavens have always attracted attention, and challenged mankind's intelligence."

Teaberry did not observe that O'Blarney was still washing glasses, then moving to the dining area to fetch even more glassware. O'Blarney was really not paying attention to the conversation. He scratched his nose, shook his head in agreement, mumbled "Uh, huh. Yeah. You know you're right about that, bub," letting Teaberry ramble. "What I need are down-to-earth experiences that will put me in focus with more mundane matters. Now that I'm retired from the conservatory, I need to plant the old feet firmly in terra firma, if you will." O'Blarney thought that Teaberry cued him for more coffee. Trying to do two things at once, he poured Teaberry's cup to the maximum and then some, spilling a steaming, black river onto his bar. He quickly wiped the liquid up, yelped, "Ouch!" when the hot bar towel dripped on his hand but, still, did not stop Teaberry's patter.

"Yeah, that's it!" Teaberry suddenly exclaimed. "I'm in California, The Sunshine State--The Gold Coast! There is plenty to see and do right here. I mean my gosh! There are Giant Sequoias; there are Spanish missions that honeycomb the coast; there are the Sierra Nevadas; there are the most beautiful parks anywhere to be found, and all this within hours of the city. That's what I'll do. Say, Mr. O'Blarney," Teaberry bubbled. "That young fellow that you speak so highly about. What's his name again?" "Huh?"

O'Blarney mumbled, still distracted by glassware. "Oh, you must mean Mizzou. Philip Mizzou is his name. What about him?" "Well," Teaberry continued, "I think that he is a fine young man. And he seems to have a fine sense of humor. You know, talking about adventure and all. And he does have an interesting mind and exceptional way to express himself. I just wonder if he, or maybe someone else from the furniture warehouse, might be interested in working for hire, as a guide into the more remote forests of this great state?" "That you'll have to ask yourself," O'Blarney replied matter of factly. "But don't count on him accepting your offer. From what I know, the young man doesn't need the money, and I doubt that he wants more side lines. He seems happy enough here--but ask him and let him speak for himself." "Fair enough then!" Teaberry said with much enthusiasm. "I can hardly wait to present my offer. Where then might I find him?" "Right here," O'Blarney replied, pointing to an empty barstool. "Right where you saw him the last time you were here. Say, if you stick around awhile, Mizzou will drop by with a friend of his from the warehouse. What's his name? Oh, yeah. Yelverton--Big John Yelverton. The two of them have been inseparable since they bought a truck. You'd think that they just won the sweepstakes. Both of them are on Cloud Nine. I guess that they want to start their own business. They'll see that it ain't so easy. If Mizzou's smart, he'll take my offer and settle down here with Mary and me. But who

knows. I was young once too, and needed the
challenge of my own place. Needed to find my own
length--my own space. Ah, whatever. We'll see,"
O'Blarney sighed, waving his arm in the air, still
holding the coffee-stained towel that had burned his
hand. Rolling the wet rag into a ball, he tossed it
into his dirty-linen bin and shuffled back to the
kitchen to check an entree in his oven. Sam's
Saturday Night Special was fried shark plank with
lemon-butter basting.

Chapter 16

E. X. Queasy fidgeted with his diet soft drink.
Rolling the glass in a massive hand, the ice cubes
clinked and rattled. Taking this as a cue to freshen
his drink, a scantily clad barmaid made her way
gingerly to the round, chrome table that he occupied
in a corner, and placed a frosty drink before him,
then softly cooed, "That will be six dollars please."
Surprised, Queasy said, "I didn't order this! Take it
away!" "But we have a two-drink minimum at
Club A-Go-Go, sir!" she protested, "and you have
been nursing that first one longer than a new-born
baby on formula. You can pay me now, or pay me

later." "Huh?" Queasy tried to protest, just as Knuckles the bouncer showed up at his table, wearing a bandage on a still-bruised forehead to cover the lumps he took tangling with Mizzou and Yelverton. "Some trouble, Babbs?" he questioned, raising his left eyebrow menacingly, and pounding a clenched fist into an open palm. "Not really," the barmaid replied. "If only this big boy will stop ogling the merchandise and start carrying his weight. He's been sucking those ice cubes for the past hour. I'm trying to tell him he has a two-drink minimum. He's got to keep drinking, or have one for the road and then scram. This ain't no mission, or lonely-heart's club. He's been eyeballing Pandora over there like he's in love or something."

"Okay, Bubbles, let's drink up or get out. You heard the lady. This ain't no social club. These dancers don't work for free, and there ain't no free lunch. Pay the lady her six bucks and keep ordering, or bounce on out of here."

Queasy's expressions turned from astonishment, to fright, to anger. He was intimidated, but hated to be bullied, and detested Knuckle's condescending, threatening style. Queasy measured his words with caution. "Boy, I'll tell you what! Hospitality in this city is for the birds. I've traveled the globe and have received better treatment, and watched better entertainment, in the Black Hole of Calcutta, India! I've seen rookie belly dancers suffering with diarrhea perform more gracefully than your Pandora. I've also seen snake charmers more gracious than any of you!"

Knuckles was not impressed. He certainly was not intimidated. "Yeah, youse and youse opinion, and a plug nickel, will get youse a bad cup of coffee down at the Union Mission. Why don't youse go down to the pier and have some bell-ringing, tuba player do the dance of the seven veils for youse!"

Babbs, the ginger barmaid, giggled. Pocketing Queasy's six dollars, she turned tail and hustled back to the bar to service her next customer. Knuckles bounced to center stage after Pandora completed her act. Extending massive arms, he helped her down the ramp, accompanied by an enthusiastic round of applause from the patronage.

Knuckles used this opportunity to express an undying devotion to Pandora. She was not impressed though. "Just keep your big paws on my arms and lay off with the beady-eyed compliments. I get enough stares, wisecracks, and cheap come ons from the sleazy Johns that you're supposedly in charge of. Who's running this joint, anyway," she bitterly complained, "the inmates or the warden? I'll tell you what, buddy boy, you missed the last sleaze ball that got fresh, didn't you? His sleazy hands were all over my derriere that last dance. And all that grief for a lousy buck!"

"Where! Show me the creep and I'll pulverize him!" Knuckles bragged. "Ahhh, you and you're big talk," Pandora shot back, "it's too late now. Just keep a better watch out the next time. I have more finger prints on me than the San Francisco cops have on file!" "Youse don't understand, baby," Knuckles tried to explain, "I was tied up with some clown in the crowd." "I don't want to hear your weak-as-water excuses," Pandora rebutted, storming toward her dressing room. "Talk is cheap!"

Knuckles stood frozen with embarrassment. Looking balefully toward Queasy, he only hoped that trouble might start so that he could vent his frustration violently.

Slamming her dressing room door, Pandora collapsed into an overstuffed easy chair that sat unimpressively in a too cluttered dressing room, servicing too many dancers. By the book, Pandora was one of the best dancers that Club A-Go-Go ever had. She never missed a day of work, the regular customers of the club all liked her, and she even enjoyed a following. Whenever she took to the stage, excitement energized the atmosphere. Drinks were purchased enthusiastically--and in abundance. She enjoyed favored status among management that labeled her a star. "Youse a star in my eyes, babe," Knuckles constantly assured her.

Kicking her patent leather, high-heeled pumps into the air, she pulled a scanty costume off a well-proportioned body, put on a robe, and breathed a deep sigh of relief. She enjoyed attention. She appreciated that on good nights the money was awesome, but at twenty-six she needed to apply herself more intelligently. Having earned BA and MA degrees from a prestigious liberal-arts college back east, she was only hours short of completing her PhD--also in liberal arts.

Her family always paid her expensive room, board, and tuition at both the undergraduate and graduate levels. Exotic dancing was mad money for her, even though her wealthy father kept her finances straight in every way. More to the point, exotic dancing was a chance for her to make a social statement, perhaps even to defy conventional wisdom of what a doctor of philosophy should be.

Her parents expected that she would assume a professorship at an ivy-covered college in the northeast. Penelope Ursula Bach, a.k.a. Pandora, was not convinced that that was what she wanted, though. Pouring a diet cola into tall, frosted glass, she took a long draw of the cool refreshment, picked up a brochure on getaway-from-it-all vacations, and thumbed through the pages. Before reading much text, though, a knock at the door startled her.

"Oh, for the love of peace and quiet! What is it now?" she protested. "Western Union, mam," a voice from the dark hallway responded. "I have a telegram for you." "A telegram?" Pandora puzzled. "No one sends telegrams anymore. Oh, alright," she finally snapped, opening the dressing room door. Grabbing the envelope from the messenger's hands, her robe popped loose, slightly exposing her bare chest. He flashed a big grin. "Sign here, please" he said, thrusting pen and paper her way. Not tipping him, Pandora complied with his request. The Western Union messenger did not mind, if indeed he even realized, that he'd been stiffed. Saying,

"Thanks, lady, and have a greeeat evening," he turned on his heels and bolted from the hallway.

Pandora plopped back into the overstuffed easy chair and tore open the telegram. It read: Daughter. Have not heard from you since the start of the term. Please write or call. You have not returned our letters. Don't know your work phone. Got your business address from the registrar's office. What is a Club A-Go-Go? Is it anything like Arthur Murray? Your mother and I tripped to the light fantastic splendidly, shortly before you were born. We miss you very much! Please call collect! Love, Mother and Father.

Pandora brushed a tear from her eye and took another drink of diet cola. She intended not to ignore her parents, only to assert her independence. Being self-sufficient meant that she need not correspond frequently, or telephone much either. During four years as an undergraduate, she was the devoted student--the faithful daughter. Joining every right club, and running in the best circles at the best school, assured her of making the right contacts. Top grades assured that she qualified for graduate school. Her father paying the burdensome annual tuition eased any pressure to make financial ends meet.

Penelope Ursula Bach certainly had no problem making academic ends meet. Her parents bragged to friends that "her intelligence challenged genius." She folded the telegram slowly and placed it carefully in her purse, vowing to write home at the next opportunity.

A second knock at her dressing room door was no more welcome than the first one. "Jumping Jehoshaphat, who is it!" she wailed, hurling her soft drink across the room, spilling cola, and shattering glass against the wall. "It's just me, babe," the low, masculine voice implored, "I just wanted to tell youse that youse a star. Youse the best." Pandora always resented intrusions of privacy from whatever quarter. She wasted no time, and minced no words with Knuckles. "Listen beans for brains. I'm in no mood for your mealy-mouthed, put your hands to- gether gents for Pandora malarkey. I've told you before, just keep the creeps out of my hair. If you really want to lavish praise upon me, send me a telegram. Now leave, and if you don't, I'm complaining to management!" "Sure, babe, but youse the best," Knuckles repeated, before walking away in despair.

E. X. Queasy did not enjoy the other dancers any more than Pandora. What really brought him to Club A-Go-Go was the attempt to locate Philibert Sandbar, and if not him, then someone from the defunct warehouse that knew of his whereabouts.

Queasy had business with Sandbar. He heard through the grapevine that drivers and their helpers frequented Club A-Go-Go and, if he got lucky, maybe someone would steer him toward Sandbar. Sandbar owed Queasy a lot of money. So much money in fact, that if Queasy did not locate Sandbar soon, he would offer a reward for information about his location.

Queasy heard that Sandbar stiffed a lot of creditors in court and skated unscathed, but Sandbar owed Queasy nearly five-hundred thousand in cash money and, by hook or crook, or whatever else it took, Queasy was not to be fleeced.

Knuckles reappeared just in time to catch Queasy's attention. He itched for a confrontation with anyone, after Pandora trashed his ego, because taking things personally cursed his flawed nature. He was not smart enough, nor sophisticated enough, to realize that Pandora loved to bash male egos. That was yet another reason she took the job as stripper. Bashing male egos was the ready-made defense for a lifestyle that invited male aggression. To her it provided the perfect cover to get cheap thrills while deflating male machismo. She did not like Knuckles, but meant nothing personal with the put downs.

"Say, young man, over here," Queasy gestured to Knuckles. "Huh, youse want me?" the bouncer asked, putting a massive right hand onto his chest. "Yes, Queasy replied, "I have a business proposition for you that might prove very lucrative to all parties involved." "Well, if youse mean that I can make some fast bucks I'm all for that," Knuckles beamed, "but mind you, I don't come cheap. I have lots of girlfriends here, and like to buy them real nice things. So I don't work for no peanuts."

"What I will offer you should be most satisfactory," Queasy offered proudly. "Just give me your undivided attention and I'm certain that you'll be much the happier when our little discussion is finished, provided, of course, that you have the wherewithal to help me." "Youse be surprised how much help I can be," the bouncer responded sharply. "Try me!"

Chapter 17

Finished with the muffler job, Yelverton was calling it a day. "Mizzou, my man, I think we're onto something really big here. Really big." Washing his face with industrial-strength soap removed all the soot from a very dirty face. "Now that I've finished the undercarriage, I'll check the brake linings, tires, and finish the mechanical go-around with the electrical system and engine. I overhauled this bad-boy's power plant just last year, but I did that for Sandbar on his piss-poor paycheck. Now that the buck stops here," Yelverton stressed, pointing an index finger at his big feet, "I intend to do the job better. Mizzou, I'm telling you, you won't recognize this thing when I'm through. With the paint job I've planned, I'll turn this once sorry buckle of bolts into a world-class wonder."

"Are we staying within budget?" Mizzou quizzed. "You know that money doesn't grow on trees. If this project costs too much, we might be better off just buying a new rig!" Yelverton laughed. "Mizzou, you book-smart egghead. You still don't know the difference between the real and make-believe world, do you? A new rig would run us at least ten times what we bought this for. Your part of the investment is just paying for materials. My time is your time, and our time translates to labor that we don't pay someone else up front with inflated charges, for work that I do better to begin with! Just because Sandbar paid us slave wages doesn't mean that everyone works for a hand shake and a smile." "Yeah, okay, mister-know-it-all," Mizzou snapped, "but just you wait until the money starts to roll in, and you don't know a debit from a credit. When you're scratching your backside for mental inspiration, the kid here will be taking care of the accounts receivable, and the accounts payable, with enough left over for a hefty profits versus losses accounting session."

Yelverton wanted to say something smart, instead settling for, "I bet you that when the chips are down, all we really need to be is in the black and out of the red. With that in mind, we'll really be in the pink!"

Climbing onto Yelverton's Harley Davidson motorcycle, the newest partnership to spring upon the San Francisco bay area headed for O'Blarney's. Revving the cycle's engine to maxed rpms, Yelverton shouted, "Hold on there, Mizzou, I can taste those sweet brews already! Line 'em up Sam, the drinks are on me tonight!"

Sam O'Blarney always served fried shark plank Saturday nights at his place. For those too conservative in taste to order this delicacy, though, he also offered deep-fried prawns, lobster, crab meat, and a full selection of steaks and chops. Yelverton was probably the best customer that O'Blarney had. Never a day passed that Yelverton did not stop for either lunch or dinner. Running a weekly tab, Yelverton was always careful to pay his bill in full, never allowing charges to exceed one-hundred dollars. Other ex-Fly By Nighters were not so conscientious. Even though most ran up bar tabs that O'Blarney kept from exceeding fifteen or twenty bucks per man, with the furniture warehouse closed, he extended more credit to regulars. A few hundred dollars was owed him.

After a couple of beers, and a two-inch thick T-bone steak with crinkle-cut fries, Yelverton was feeling pretty good. "Say, my man," he told Mizzou, "we could do us some public relations work here and pay off the accounts of some of these boys." "Huh," Mizzou protested, "there you go again. We can't afford that! Thought you wanted to be in the black! Already we're losing money!" "Just you never mind, my man," Yelverton drawled, "look at old shorty over there." "Smythe?" Mizzou waxed, "He's the biggest dead beat I've ever known! I've bought more drinks for him than I care to remember! He still owes me for the last time we were here!"

Slumped over a beer in the tavern's farthest corner, Smythe looked like he just lost his life--not his job. His limp body mimicked death. A calloused red hand clutched a beer, like a lobster hooking its catch; his eyes were glazed. "Hello, anybody home?" Yelverton asked, laughing, waving a huge right arm before Smythe's face to get attention. Smythe did not respond. "Hello! Good buddy! Hey, Smythe! It's me! Yelverton! Wake up, and join the living!"

Shaking Smythe vigorously produced some result--however slow. "Huh, uh, yeah!" Smythe snapped, obviously disoriented, still feeling the effects of too many beers in too little time. Rubbing his red face, Smythe tried to bring himself around. "Hey, Sam, bring me another beer!" Smythe ordered. "Cancel that beer and bring Smythe a steaming hot coffee!" Yelverton countered. "Smythe, you don't need more booze, you need a job!" "Huh, a job?" Smythe asked. "Oh, I've lost my job no thanks to Sandbar. Fly By Night Van Lines was my life--my home away from home. Thanks to Sandbar pissing away the business, a lot of good men have no work these days. I'm mad!"

O'Blarney set hot coffee before Smythe then left slowly, saying, "Sober up, Smythe, it ain't all that bad, I might be able to help out a little. Forget the money that you owe me. If you need work I could use an extra bartender now and then." "Thanks, Sam, you're all heart," Smythe gushed, pounding his chest and making the sourest of faces with the boozy movements of someone too drunk to think straight. "My friend Yelverton needs another drink. Sam, give him whatever he wants and put it on my tab!" "Cancel those drinks," Yelverton ordered. "Sam, bring us a pot of black coffee and another cup. Smythe and I have a lot of talking to do. On second thought, Sam, make that two more cups and a bigger pot of black coffee. Hey Mizzou! My man, over here!" Yelverton called, gesturing for his partner to join the table, "business meeting, on the double!"

"Tell Smythe here that we think a lot of him," Yelverton told Mizzou immediately after pouring coffee into all cups. Continuing, he added, "Go on, my man, tell Smythe what you were telling me awhile ago...that he's the MVP of the furniture business, and a VIP to boot. Go on, Mizzou, tell him that he's more the furniture man than you or me put together. Tell him!"

Mizzou looked incredulously at Yelverton. Trying to sound persuasive, he wasn't. "Yeah, Smythe," Mizzou lied, "I was just telling old Yelverton here that you were very underrated and never appreciated by Sandbar. He, uh, took you for granted, you know, used you. But then Sandbar did that to everyone. You know that Sandbar used the business as a front to smuggle drugs didn't you?" Smythe still was not coherent. "Huh? No, I don't recall a Doug. Doug who?" he asked. "No, listen Smythe!" Mizzou continued, "Drugs! Sandbar was selling drugs, and that's why the business went to hell in a handbasket. All Sandbar really wanted was his money up front. It must be that. I saw him with my own two eyes that day we moved E. X. Queasy. Sandbar took a package from his briefcase, handed it to Queasy, then Queasy handed over a lot of cash. You know, the crisp kind that banks wrap with brown bands. I saw a hell of a lot of money but, at the time, Sandbar just made it look like a furniture deal. After our bizarre experience that day, I figured that Sandbar sold drugs and, for sure, Queasy was a user, or at least a dealer, too."

"Yeah, maybe," Smythe replied, sobering from several cups of coffee. "But why the dirty dealing with his employees and, why stop now?" "Because he was treading on very thin ice," Mizzou said slowly. "You know Sandbar better than I do, but chances are the DEA was watching him and still is. All Sandbar really had left to option was closing the business in a rush and getting the hell out of Dodge City. That's exactly what he did. Have you, has anyone for that matter, seen him since the auction?" Mizzou always asked the right questions at the right time.

"Then you're telling me that I was working for a drug dealer and not a furniture man?" Smythe concluded, finally putting two and two together. "Yeah, that's exactly what I'm telling you," Mizzou replied, "and further, Sandbar took all of his cash money from drugs or whatever he could skim from the business and bolted!" "You've already said that,

Mizzou!" Yelverton waxed. "Old Smythe here might be gassed to the gills but he ain't stupid!" Smythe tried to swish the coffee in his cup. Still too woozy to coordinate his movements, he spilled it.

Yelverton used this opportunity to express ideas to Smythe. "Now that Mizzou told you that, you know as much as we do about the Fly By Night business, but that's history. Now listen, Smythe, what brought us all together for this little business meeting is this." Yelverton measured his words carefully, relishing the moment that he, as entrepreneur, always wanted. Now Yelverton was a business owner, had a partner, and might very soon become a boss. "Smythe, Mizzou and me have our own trucking company you know, and we'll need some help. Are you interested?"

This presentation caught Mizzou by surprise. He did not appreciate Yelverton making him a silent partner in their venture, let alone Big John making decisions without first consulting him. But he maintained silence. Smythe was slow to respond, but understood. "You're offering me a job, aren't you?" he finally said. "Yeah, that's it exactly," Yelverton affirmed, "you always caught on fast, Smythe." Mizzou scratched his head, wondering how they would pay Smythe, since they had no business lined up. Then Mizzou broke into the conversation. "Bear in mind that this is an initial proposal, Smythe. Yelverton is just sending out feelers, you know, to see who is or isn't interested." Mizzou frowned at Yelverton and continued, "Of course, you're our very first pick for extra help, though we can't start you out at the money that Sandbar paid, as business increases, we might boost your pay."

Smythe didn't wait long before responding, "Yeah, I'll take you both up on the offer. I'll work for O'Blarney as a bartender until things pick up with the trucking business. If I start for O'Blarney soon, I can still make ends meet. Yeah, things are starting to gel again."

No more than finished saying that, Smythe was surprised when O'Blarney presented him with the Saturday Night Special--fried shark plank. "Gee, thanks, Sam," Smythe gushed. "Don't mention it," O'Blarney replied, "I'm trying a new seasoning for the dish: An epicurean-type-food-critic opinion from you, when done, shall be appreciated." Smythe dug into his entree with voracious appetite.

Chapter 18

E. X. Queasy finished his business with Knuckles the bouncer, then left Club A-Go-Go. Pandora's presence upon the stage, for her last performance of the night, created the expected air of excitement.

Drinks were selling briskly. Queasy slid behind the wheel of his posh Bugatti Royale Coupe Napoleon roadster and, under neon splash, left for the streets of San Francisco. The vehicle was a priceless beauty of orange and gold, sporting a silver elephant dancing upon a chrome radiator cap.

Driving with what he perceived as usual defensive caution, he observed all rules of the road. Stopping at every red light, driving within the allowable speed, and using his turn signal whenever he changed lanes, Queasy was surprised to look into his rear-view mirror and spot the flashing blue light of a motorcycle cop.

"What the...," he whispered to himself, pulling the golden-gate-orange automobile to the curb, "I haven't done anything!" Walking menacingly to Queasy's sleek roadster, the motorcycle cop calmly said, "May I see your driver's license, insurance, and proof of ownership, please." "Sure, officer, no problem," Queasy replied, handing his paperwork out the window. "May I ask what the stop is for. Is this a routine check or what?" The cop did not answer, but looked long and hard at Queasy's credentials. Finally the cop answered. "We've had a rash of stolen vehicles lately. The economy you know. These exotic models are particularly attractive. I'm just doing my job and trying to keep insurance premiums down. All right, Dr. Queasy. Your paperwork is in order. I'm satisfied that you check out. You're free to go, and drive carefully."

Queasy did not bother putting his paperwork back

into his glove box. Visibly shaken, he hastily stuffed everything into his jacket pocket, waited momentarily for the motorcycle cop to speed away, then drove into traffic. Breathing a sigh of relief, he considered himself lucky that everything checked out with the SFPD cop. Near Praesidio, though, Queasy lowered his guard. Approaching a traffic signal, and still flustered, he hesitated when the light went yellow from green. With the signal red, he gambled that he would beat book. He didn't see any SFPD units about, so what were the odds of being stopped twice in one night?

Queasy should have stopped. Before he got past the intersection, blue lights flashed into his rear-view mirror. Again Queasy pulled his Bugatti to the curb. He recognized the same motorcycle cop. "Huh," Queasy protested, "you again?" "You ran a red light, sir. I was behind you and sped up to see you blow the light. Now. May I see your driver's license, please!" Producing the necessary document, Queasy sat nervously looking into his rear-view mirror at the SFPD motorcycle cop. He could not believe what had happened. Twenty-five years behind the wheel and never a moving violation. Now lightning struck twice the same night. The motorcycle cop returned to Queasy's window. Handing the disappointed motorist a yellow ticket, it of newspaper texture, he said, "Your court date is printed underneath the explanation of charges. This is not an admission of guilt, only that you are charged with running the red light. Sign on the dotted line please." Queasy quickly scribbled his name. "What about my driver's license?" "You pick that up the day you tell it to the judge," the cop replied. "See you there." "Uh, yeah, Officer uuuh...," "Saxon," the officer replied, "Sergeant Aloysius Saxon."

Queasy was not driving about San Francisco aimlessly. His destination was O'Blarney's Inn. He had unfinished business with Philibert Sandbar and, knowing that most of the warehouse workers frequented Sam's place, Queasy played a hunch that either Sandbar, or information about him, could be found there. Queasy bounced into Sam's and parked his massive body in a booth overlooking the parking lot. Looking through a pane-glass window, Queasy admired the sleek brilliance of his Bugatti roadster. Ill-gotten gains provided him with the finest luxuries that money could buy. Mizzou was right. Queasy dealt with Sandbar buying and selling illegal drugs. But what Mizzou did not know was that Sandbar had involved himself with much more.

Sandbar had unwittingly made acquaintance with the world's best counterfeiter. Queasy used Sandbar's business to smuggle some of the best plates ever made for counterfeiting fifty US dollar and five-hundred French franc denominations. Sandbar's connection to Fly By Night Van Lines, and his overseas contacts in Zurich, custom tailored the needs of E. X. Queasy, a.k.a. Jean-Luc LaPierre.

When first dealing dirty with Queasy, Philibert Sandbar's eyes grew bigger even than the green

78

ovals of past presidents; his smoking cigar dropped amidst red-hot sparks; but clammy hands greedily grasped the crisp roll of fresh bills thrust at him to consummate a deal. Queasy intended only to test the waters by buying the street drugs that Sandbar offered. With success assured, he would take delivery of the plates secreted within the Zelman and Zelda Unger shipment, pay Sandbar the rest of the money upon delivery, and be done with the whole affair.

But Queasy underestimated Sandbar's cunning. He even miscalculated the crisis which Sandbar lived under far, far too long. He didn't factor that Sandbar might rifle the Unger shipment, then plunder the counterfeit money that was secreted there. The Ungers were ideal. They were randomly selected, and used, for their San Francisco destination. Mizzou, meanwhile, had no clue that his hideaway was a red-hot stash of phony cash.

Now Sandbar had the bogus dollars crammed into a briefcase bound for Switzerland. He planned to open a no-questions-asked bank account there. But he didn't know that the money was counterfeit. Queasy just told him that, "A large sum of undeclared drug funds was coming into the country." Nor did Queasy tell Sandbar about the best plates that Interpol ever pinched. Counterfeit French francs alerted them to the scam. But the plates eluded them, and now the plates eluded Queasy. He needed to find Sandbar desperately.

Chapter 19

"Wake up sir!" the gate attendant implored, shaking Sandbar vigorously until the groggy little man opened his eyes and sprang to his feet, not knowing where he was or what was happening. Continuing, the petite woman said, "Your non-stop flight to New York's International Airport, continuing on to Zurich, Switzerland, has already boarded. I've taken the liberty of checking you in. Here is your boarding pass with seating assignment. Your flight will be leaving very shortly." "Huh, yeah, thanks!" Sandbar blurted, tucking his ever-present briefcase under arm before bolting for the boarding ramp. "You make flying at night a great pleasure. This is Saturday night, isn't it?" he asked yawning, rubbing his eyes with a free hand. The attendant nodded in agreement. "I see now why they call this flight the red-eye express. What time are we to arrive in New York?" he puzzled. "Weather permitting about six a.m. Eastern Time, tomorrow. Enjoy the flight!"

Finished with her good deed for the day, the gate attendant signaled the flight attendants that the last passenger was aboard. Closing the cabin door behind Sandbar, the flight attendant directed the sleepy little man to his first-class seat. Before placing his oxblood briefcase underneath it, Sandbar double checked its contents to ensure that his fresh cash was inside. The counterfeit US dollars and French francs, in denominations of fifty and five-hundred, were still neatly stacked beneath his boxes of Havana Golden Wand cigars. Smiling, Sandbar closed the rich, leather briefcase, then locked the clasp with a small key that fit neatly into his pocket. Turning to catch the attendant's eye, Sandbar spoke quickly. "Miss, I'm not interested in refreshments or food this flight. I always eat before leaving for the airport. Stomach disorder, you know. What I hope to enjoy is uninterrupted peace and quiet." "Very well, then. But understand that this is a long flight. We'll serve beverages and a full meal before arriving in New York. You'll be very hungry," she cautioned patronizingly. "We do have special menus from which to choose for those with medical needs." "Thanks," Sandbar burped, "but I meant what I said. I've flown Sky Bus Airways before, and your food ain't nothing to brag about anyway. Please, if I fall asleep, don't wake me up!" "Very well, sir," the flight attendant said coldly, "but don't say that...," "Yeah, yeah, yeah," Sandbar blabbed.

The passenger sitting beside Sandbar laughed, then tugged at the bill of his cap. In black lettering upon a yellow field it read, CAT. Butting into the conversation he gushed, "I'm hungry enough to eat a bear, little lady! Say, bring me this fellow's tray and

I'll save it for a snack on down the road. I'm not one to waste food, or to turn my nose up at chow already paid for." "I'll do that, then," the attendant replied, walking toward the galley to prepare for the beverage disbursement.

"What's the name, partner? Mine is Harry Hart," the affable man inquired, extending a hand for Sandbar to shake. "Wilbur. Wilbur Wright," Sandbar sarcastically lied, wanting only to sleep. "Say, fancy that!" the passenger laughed, "that's a perfect name for flying. Any relation?" Sandbar said only, "No, no relation." Reaching for the in-flight magazine tucked into the seat before him, he pretended to read, while thinking that his seatmate looked vaguely familiar. Sandbar's seatmate took the cue and directed his attention to the voice coming over the intercom. "Ladies and gentlemen, this is Captain Orville Wright." Amidst laughter he continued, "And no relation, unfortunately. We will be cruising at an altitude of twenty-eight thousand feet, at a speed of five hundred and fifty miles per hour. We may experience some turbulence later in the flight so please don't be alarmed. We shall keep you posted. Our estimated time of arrival is six a.m. Eastern Time. I hope that you enjoy your flight and thank you for flying Sky Bus Airways!"

Take off was operationally smooth. With the FASTEN YOUR SEATBELT sign blinking off, the flight attendants efficiently disbursed drinks. At this point Sandbar--magazine spread across his rotund belly--was asleep or pretending to be, and completely missed the affable passenger next to him quaffing drinks with both hands. The attendant gave him Sandbar's drinks--per order. All passengers were enjoying a most comfortable flight, and Sandbar was oblivious to everything, as sleep finally came. By the time the attendants served another snack--this to include sandwiches--a hungry Harry Hart ravenously downed one club sandwich and was tearing into the next. Sandbar was dead to the world. Snoring softly, he looked comfortable in his own little world.

The turbulence of which Captain Wright spoke eventually presented itself. While munching club sandwiches, the passengers were presented with a message. "Ladies and gentlemen, as mentioned at take off, we are experiencing clear air turbulence. We in the industry call this phenomenon a CAT. Such conditions are not uncommon this time of year, and certainly not for our location. If you will look out below, you will note that we are sailing majestically high above the Rocky Mountains even as I speak. We should weather this with no major problem, but for your safety, please observe the no smoking and fasten your seatbelt signs and, once again, thanks for flying Sky Bus Airways!"

The huge aircraft flew uneventfully through mild turbulence, but eventually took several violent jolts, mixing the on-board atmosphere with surprise and muffled cries. Babies screamed, children screeched, men and women shouted for attendants. Sandbar was roused to consciousness with the 747 rocking violently. "Huh? Jumping Jehoshaphat! What's happening?" he cried, springing to his feet and banging his head against the luggage rack. "Ouch!" he protested, thoroughly disoriented. "Sir!" a flight attendant, snapped, "you weren't listening to Captain Wright! We are just experiencing a CAT. Please sit down and fasten you seat belt!" "To blazes with my seatbelt!" Sandbar snapped back. "I'm heading for the men's room. My stomach can't take all this churning!"

He grabbed his briefcase and tucked it protectively under an arm. "Sir!" the attendant protested, springing to her feet. "You aren't allowed out of your seat when the red light is flashing...please sit back down!" "Say again," Sandbar insisted, "my guts are about to spill up all over the place. I paid for my seat, and if I want my seat to be a toilet seat, I'll head to the men's room. Bye!" Before the attendant could reach Sandbar, he hustled to the toilet. Slamming the flimsy door shut, he snapped the latch into place. He looked into his briefcase. Satisfied that the cash was undisturbed, he plopped onto the toilet, reached into his pocket for his antacid tablets, popped a handful into his mouth and chewed noisily. He took a shot of coffee liqueur from his silver flask to wash the mess down. Then he took another shot, and then another. He finished the flask and saw in the mirror that the color had returned to his face. With the flight attendant banging upon the door, he decided to give in and return to his seat. But he intended to complain to Sky Bus management in New York.

Slowly opening the door, Sandbar saw that the attendant was busying herself with excited passengers, but spotted him in time to issue an ultimatum. "Sir," I've about had it up to here with you! Now go to your seat and fasten your belt! Pleeease!" Still sleepy, nauseous, and confused, Sandbar flew into a rage. Charging forward in the cabin, he was on top of the frightened attendant, cursing and waving his arms in patented Fly-By-Night fashion. His briefcase tucked snugly under his left arm, Sandbar rocked violently as the 747 encountered CAT after CAT. "I'm reporting you and your CAT to management, and I'm reporting management to the CAB or the FAA! Let them deal with your CAT!" "Sir, very well then. You win! Please take your seat and we'll put your report on our comment card." "Stuff your comment card," Sandbar blurted, suddenly rocked and thrown violently against the emergency exit, "I...," but before he finished, the door's crash bar gave, and with the 747 dipping violently down and left, the emergency door flew open and sucked him into night's cold sky. The door slamming shut with a whooosh guaranteed that Sandbar could not hear the scream of a startled flight attendant. Falling through the frigid sky toward the Rocky Mountains below, Sandbar spun and tumbled, his cigar and cash scattered to the winds. "Helllp! he cried, with Captain Orville Wright and Sky Bus Airway's 747 vanishing into icy darkness.

Chapter 20

Sam O'Blarney tended personally to the needs of his customers. He had not seen Queasy before, yet judging by the hefty proportions of this newest diner, O'Blarney thought that Queasy's appetite must be good and, therefore, he should order robustly. O'Blarney was right. Greeting Queasy he said with affection, "This is a fine Saturday night, now isn't it." Placing an enormous chinaware platter, and table setting, gingerly upon the table he continued, "Our Saturday night special is shark plank with a very delightful lemon-butter basting. Please try some!" "My good man," Queasy bragged, "I have dined in the finest restaurants throughout the world. I have sampled every kind of seafood to include fried octopus, and whale meat. I have heard of shark meat delighting some, but then one needs the taste buds for that, uh, delicacy. I'm sorry, no offense meant, but I shall pass on shark though, please, bring me a shrimp cocktail appetizer for starters because, boy, am I famished! Include a surf and turf platter as the main course, with a side order of deep fried mushrooms. I had my limit of libations earlier, at a very dumpy nightclub, so a pot of your blackest coffee will do me fine. Oh, and one other thing," he whispered, slipping a crisp five dollar bill into O'Blarney's right hand, "Perhaps some information. Tell me where I might find Philibert Sandbar."

O'Blarney looked at Queasy from the corner of his eye and blurted, "What's with the hush-hush attitude? We have no secrets here! Sandbar have some unpaid parking tickets besides his other disasters, or what? Say, you aren't a private copper or something! Or just a wise guy, maybe?"

O'Blarney was very protective of Fly By Nighters. He continued, "But I'll ask around with some of the boys. Keep in mind, though, that five dollars will not buy a lot of information." Queasy winked and returned, "Don't worry about that, if the surf and turf is to my liking, and bear in mind that I have eaten the finest lobster and steak in the world's greatest restaurants, then money is no object. My tip, to insure prompt service, shall also tell I pay well for tips of a verbal kind. Now please, without further ado, my shrimp cocktail!"

O'Blarney shuffled over to Mizzou's table. "See that big gentleman over there, noshing on my bread sticks like there's no tomorrow. Well, he just slipped me a five spot to tell him where he might find Sandbar. Hell, I don't know where he is. Sandbar only stopped in now and then, but I told the guy that I'd ask around. If any of you know anything, I'll pass it on to him."

Finished--with right thumb pointing over his right shoulder toward Queasy's table--O'Blarney shuffled toward the kitchen to present Queasy's order. O'Blarney had customers, and then he had customers that came in for more than a good meal. Sam O'Blarney wasn't sure that he liked Queasy, but he would wait to get reactions from the ex-furniture men before he passed judgment.

"Say, Mizzou, I have a memory for faces, and with your mind for names and dates, doesn't that turkey look mighty familiar?" Yelverton asked, pointing his massive right arm Queasy's way. With Queasy spreading a pat of golden butter on a bread stick, and munching away oblivious to everything but the need to feed his fat face, Mizzou looked over his shoulder and replied, "Well, what do you know about that! Look, Smythe, the big fat guy over there. That's E. X. Queasy. The fellow that got Yelverton fired and, I suspect, was dealing dirty-drug business with Sandbar."

"Huh?" Smythe yawned, still sobering from too many beers, but not enough coffee in him to fully comprehend the situation, "Uh, yeah. The question. Right. I'll work for both of you starting day after tomorrow. That's Monday, right?" "Wrong!" Mizzou replied. "That's not question but Queasy. E. X. Queasy! He's the fellow that loaded up his brownies with hallucinogenic drugs. You remember the day that I had the funny experience? You did too...right Yelverton?" Mizzou made a sarcastic face. Sticking both thumbs into his ears he waved his hands mockingly.

Big John fumed, "I was so mad that day I must have walked for miles before heading for the warehouse. There I crashed on some furniture pads, fell asleep waiting for Sandbar, and the next thing I knew it was morning. I saw Sandbar, cussed him out, picked up my pay, and left. That's the last I saw of him until the auction. But wait," Yelverton sighed, scratching his head and looking deep in thought. "That night at the warehouse I did have a strange dream. At least I think that it was a dream. Sandbar was climbing all over one twenty-three, you know, like he was looking for something. It had to be a dream. I mean, Mizzou, does that count as a funny experience?"

"You're sure that you were dreaming and not just disoriented?" Mizzou asked. "You know, it is possible that Sandbar was there that night. If he was into the drug scene, then he would do that business at very odd hours, and the Queasy job was that day. It follows that he would be in the truck, or at least around the truck, or furniture in storage, if he wanted to keep a handle on hidden drugs." "Anything's possible," Yelverton replied, but the bottom line is, do we want to tell that fat bastard that we have no idea where Sandbar is; or do we simply ignore him and tell him nothing, and hope he goes away!" "I'll tell you this," Mizzou cautioned. "Now that we know Sandbar's real action, and think that Sandbar's on the run, we can bet that el fatso over there has serious business with him. And further, the DEA is probably looking over both their shoulders. I say we tell Sam that nobody knows nothing--period!"

O'Blarney served Queasy a full and glorious surf and turf platter. Splitting the rock-lobster tail, then dipping the morsel into a crock of hot butter, Queasy wasted little time thanking Sam. "My deepest compliments to the chef!" the gourmand bubbled. "I have enjoyed cuisine throughout the world, and this ranks with the finest that I have ever tasted. The shrimp cocktail was out of this world!"

Queasy cut deeply into his New York Strip with razor-sharp knife, gorged himself with a bloody-red chunk of corn-fed beef, and exclaimed patronizingly, "Mr. Sam, this is the most tender piece of beef that I have ever enjoyed. Your restaurant is tops. World class! The food, the service, the ambiance is unquestionably without equal. I look forward to dessert!"

"Well, we are known for our ice-cream sundaes. The fudge topping is our own special home-made secret and Mary, my wife, has a brownie garnish that folks rave about." "Say no more Mr. Sam," Queasy oozed, "you're giving me goose bumps. How ever did you know that I am a chocoholic? I'll have a double ice-cream sundae with chocolate ice cream and, please, sprinkle some chocolate shavings upon the whipped topping." "You've got it!" O'Blarney replied, "One brown ice-cream sundae double deluxe with wings."

Entering the kitchen, O'Blarney called out to his

wife. "Mary, we have us a real gourmet deluxe tonight! This big order says we make the best seafood and beef platter going, then he orders our gut-buster-royale dessert. I'm loading him up. Cut me a couple wedges of your brownies, dear. I think that this guy is going to spread the cash around tonight!"

Returning to Queasy's table, O'Blarney set the sparkling dessert before the bubbling fat man and explained away the sensational fireworks. "I hope that you don't mind the sparklers, but my wife talked me into it. Normally, we only dress up birthday cakes, but on special occasions, or when I have an unusual request like I did for the double-deluxe sundae, well, we like to do things up brown. You'll also notice that we included an extra fudge brownie."

Queasy could not contain himself. "The entire meal has been a ceremony fit for royalty!" he exploded. "Mr. Sam, you are without equal! Now I only hope that you might deliver the information that I seek." "Uh, yeah, information," O'Blarney sighed, rubbing chocolate sauce from his left forearm. "I'll let you finish your meal and then tell you what I know, okay?" "Mr. Sam, you are precious," Queasy purred, scooping the ice-cream sundae into his cavernous mouth. "I'm indebted to you, and the tip shall reflect my appreciation. I haven't had this much fun since last July fourth. I just love pyrotechnics!" "Yeah, enjoy," Sam O'Blarney beamed, a broad smile filling his face, "and I'll tell my wife how pleased you are. She always appreciates compliments."

Queasy shoveled the frosty, gooey dessert ravenously into his plump face. His cheeks puffed and his eyes bulged with every spoonful. O'Blarney relayed Queasy's compliments-to-the-chief and, presenting himself again to Mizzou's table said, "Well, what's the verdict? Does anyone know anything?" "No way!" Mizzou insisted. "We have a consensus. Sandbar has gone underground, no doubt about that, but we don't know where, and really don't care. Brush that big blimp off however you want, just don't send him over here!"

O'Blarney took Queasy's check to the cash register and, returning to his table, gave him change. "Thank you so much again!" Queasy burst, slipping a crisp twenty dollar bill into O'Blarney's hand, "This little token ought to express my appreciation for a most delicious experience. Now, about that information I wanted." O'Blarney frowned and said, "Yeah, I'm sorry to have to say that I can't tell you a thing, because I asked around and nobody knows a thing. I can't deliver when there's nothing to deliver, and I won't lie. Sorry."

The smile on Queasy's face dissolved to a sour stare. "I don't understand," he protested. "You seemed to think that someone knew something...at least...." "Now just a minute!" O'Blarney blurted, "I promised to ask around, and I did. You just had a hell of a good meal. One of the best ever by your own admission, so let's not spoil what otherwise was a magical culinary adventure. Huh?"

Chapter 21

Sgt. Aloysius Saxon buzzed the streets of San
Francisco for one half hour after Queasy's ticket,
then headed for the police station. He liked
patrolling the streets, even if that was not his duty
assignment. Actually, he was an undercover
investigator for the DEA. Since Queasy was seen
often with Sandbar, either on a social or business
level, the DEA placed Queasy under surveillance
too, because Sandbar already was under their
thumb. Further, the DEA figured that in an
orchestrated, sting effort, they might land several
big fish in the same net. Sandbar was one of the
West Coast's known "big fishes"--Saxon did not yet
realize how big Queasy would become.
   Pulling into the SFPD precinct garage--that
doubled as the Drug Enforcement Agency sting
headquarters--Saxon parked his Harley Davidson
Electra Glide motorcycle, pausing to smoke a
cigarette, before heading up the concrete steps to his
noisy office. The garage was a beehive of activity
on a Saturday night. Squad car's tires squealed with

each departure and arrival. Arrests were easy to make on weekends. Boozers, dopers, perverts, and brawlers came to the police. Bringing violators in was easier than snagging a tuna from a slow boat in the bay.

At moments like this, Aloysius Saxon relished his job. Twenty years in law enforcement, with award presentation upon award presentation, assured him a storied reputation among those fighting crime in the bay area. He was what many called the "cop's cop." He was also a Sergeant First Class in the Army Reserve. His friends called him Sarge."

"Hey Saxon!" a voice called, echoing about the garage like a pistol shot in the night. "The commander wants to have a word with you about you know who. Seems he can't take his mind off this case one minute. He's upstairs pacing right now. You'd think he was an expectant father in a maternity ward for gosh sake!" "Yeah, thanks Zzyzzx," Saxon returned. "Just let me finish my smoke and I'll be along. Tell old blubber butt to sit tight. Tell him I'm finishing up some last-minute paperwork or something. I'm not complaining, but you know him. Whenever we're hot on some stiff's trail, he dogs you to death. Lets us do the dirty work while he pushes papers, gets ulcers, but always takes the lion's share of glory. I'll be there when I get there!" "All right, man, but don't keep the old man waiting!" Zzyzzx barked, before turning and bolting up the concrete stairwell--door slamming with a booom!

"Jumping Jehoshaphat! Save me from backstabbing, brown-nosing, butt kissers like him!" Saxon muttered. "One of these days! One of these days!" he hissed, shaking his fist in the air, then pitching his cigarette to the deck, crushing it beneath his shiny boot, "I am going to lose it and send that bastard Zzyzzx into The Twilight Zone. One thing I can't stand is a company spy!"

Saxon entered the precinct offices. Slamming his white motorcycle helmet onto a table, he walked toward the glass enclosure that served as home-away-from-home for Commander Zelman Unger "I wish that you'd tell that mealy-mouthed so and so to mind his own business!" Saxon complained. "You know that I'm the hardest working man you have in the DEA. I don't need that son-of-a-bitch poking his nose up my rear every time I leave this place. He was hiding in some corner waiting for me the moment that I drove up. Damn it! He's worse than some rookie that gets under foot, or worse yet, some firehouse dog that craps all over, letting you clean the mess up right after you've stepped into it! Can't you tell him to lay off!" "Uh, right, I'll tell him to lay off," Unger lied, looking at a stack of papers on his desk. "The guy means well. It's just that he hasn't your experience. That's all" "Well, tell him to back off, okay?" Saxon implored. "We're all a little anxious for this case to break, Sarge. Settle down! Settle down!" Unger demanded. "Who's idea was this sting operation anyway?" Saxon beseeched. "Who thought to set up those moves with Fly By Night Van Lines, thinking it just a matter of time before Sandbar tripped his hand. Me, that's who. Who's idea was it to put Harry Hart on Sandbar's trail from San Francisco to Zurich and back again. Mine," Saxon insisted, slamming his open hand on Unger's desk. "You know as well as me, Commander, that we're just this close from breaking it wide open!" he crowed, holding his thumb and forefinger a half inch apart. "If Sandbar was getting drugs out of the country, then he was shipping them with his freight to Europe. And if he was bringing anything in, then maybe it came in the same way."

"Look," Unger said, "nobody doubts that you are the hardest working man in the DEA, but you are also turning into one the hardest guys to work with, and for me, one of the hardest to understand. Your plan for getting on the inside with those dummy moving jobs was a stroke of genius, and putting Hart on Sandbar's trail made our job that much easier too. We're still waiting on an update from Harry on the latest there, but the burning question I have for you now," he paused, lighting a pipeful of cherry-blend tobacco, "is this. Did you get the device planted on fats-a-rama?" "Yes, of course," Saxon said, unbuttoning his shirt, then stuffing a royal blue, clip-on tie into his pocket. "I pulled him over on a routine check, and clamped the homing device to his bumper, pretending to read his license plate. Then I tailed him and, get this, while testing the homing frequency, which works like a charm by the way, I saw him run a light, and even wrote a ticket for the realism effect. You should have seen the look on fatso's face," Saxon guffawed, "We can run a check on this guy though DEA's investigation bureau. In fact, I've already done it. One way or the other, if he is part of Sandbar's operation, or just some muscle trying to horn in on the action, having his modus operandi should help. Snatching his license for running a red light was just the nail in that fat-boy's coffin. I have a sneaking hunch that any friend of Sandbar, driving around in a classic Bugatti roadster, is a mighty fat fish just begging to be hooked."

Unger blew great clouds of smoke into the air that swirled and spun like a cob web, or pale ghost, dancing in the light. He spoke amidst clouds of gray. "Yeah, chances are there are many prize catches in this sting. The last time that we ran an operation this extensive, we shut down most of the payload coming up from South America. But you know those boys are very resourceful. All they did was set up dummy fronts in Italy and Switzerland, running the stuff through there. I'll admit. Uncovering Sandbar with Harry Hart was a brilliant move. How did you ever do it?"

Unger was a master at stroking egos. By urging Saxon to boast about his prowess, he could expand his knowledge of command decision making, and feather his nest simultaneously. Unger knew that Saxon had powerful friends --an international network of contacts. He wanted some of that action.

"Well!" Saxon burst, always eager to applaud international connections. "It was elementary really. You see, a long time ago I made friends with some of the insiders at Interpol, and they monitor the underworld closely. Anyhow, smuggling is a specialty of the European-crime scene, and they stumbled onto Sandbar, and needed a man in the states to complete the link. That's me. And the DEA. All I did was assign Hart to the case and point him to Sandbar at Fly By Night. Every time that Sandbar belched, Hart heard it. In fact, as you know, Sandbar and Hart are on their way to Zurich even as I speak, and this time I just know that we'll sit on that guy. I have this hunch that old Philibert Sandbar's luck has run out, and that Hart will be there to nail his butt to the wall."

Unger was disappointed that Saxon did not mention names inside Interpol, but Saxon was smarter at this stage of the game than Unger gave him credit for being. "Uh," Unger said, "what did you say that inspector's name was? You know, the undercover contact with Interpol. "Ah, ah, ah! Trade secret," Saxon admonished, shaking his finger at Commander Zelman Unger, while reaching for the door handle, before returning to the noise and hub bub of the precinct's outer office. "If I told you that, then the operation would not be covert, now would it?" "You know that I can order you to tell me Saxon!" Unger blurted in frustration. "No, not on your life!" Saxon rebutted. "That information is released on a need-to-know basis. You only want to steal some more of my action. I might tell you, though, when this caper is finished, or...," "Or what?" Unger snapped, "or, I might tell you if you call off your lap dog over there."

Saxon pointed toward Zzyzzx, who was making his way through the precinct with two steaming cups of coffee. One for him and one for the Commander. "I'll think about it, Saxon," Commander Unger sighed, scratching his head. "Yeah, you do that, and I'll think about it too," Saxon mocked, shuffling toward his desk.

Zzyzzx and Unger spent the better part of a slow night drinking coffee and spinning lyrical yarns about funnier aspects of their life's work. "You know, Zzyzzx, I have to hand it to old Saxon there. He coordinated this sting operation beautifully." "Yeah," Zzyzzx agreed, "but his taste in ladies leaves a lot to be desired. I think he set me up with some two-ton Hilda from the motor pool. Man, she was ten kinds of ugly! Looked like she fell out of an ugly tree and hit every branch on the way down. And the prop! We used this old upright piano that he had painted pink, and I think is still stuffed in the stairwell of some tenement walk-up. But all those jobs trying to uncover his supplier--and still nothing! The business goes bust, the main man bolts, and we sit here drinking coffee while he chases a fat man for running red lights. We might have won the battle, but we lost the war!" "This is a funny business Zzyzzx," Unger cautioned. "It ain't over 'til the fat lady sings. Something might break our way yet."

Saxon settled in for what he hoped would be a quiet night. He had paperwork to catch up on, and always enjoyed the opportunity to spend a "quiet night at the office." It reminded him of his days as a motorized SFPD cop, when he burned motorists with traffic tickets, and spent the rest of the night behind his desk--writing reports. "Here's some information for you Sarge," a voice said, breaking Saxon's concentration, but catching him in a receptive mood. "Here, read this." Saxon read with interest the bulletin placed before him. His jaw dropped and he jumped to his feet. Not bothering to knock, he burst into Commander Unger's smoke-filled office. "Have I got news for you!" he shouted, immediately capturing his boss's attention. "Well, what is it, then?" Unger demanded, fondling his smoldering pipe in his hands. "Go on, man. Shoot!"

"Brace yourself," Saxon cautioned. "The news that I have is good and bad. I'll give you the good news first." "Damn it, Saxon!" Unger snapped, "Just give it to me both barrels!" "Well, the good news is that Queasy has a lot of outstanding warrants, to include big-time counterfeiting. We got a match when we ran his photo through investigations. So we lifted a print from his license, and we got another match through Interpol. Seems E. X. Queasy is also known as Jean-Luc La Pierre, one of the best counterfeiters in the business. We have us one of the main players in international bad paper. Interpol thinks that he's sitting on some of the best plates ever forged. They were about to alert us to watch for this bird anyway." "And what's the bad news might I ask?" Unger implored, "I hate suspense." "The bad news," Saxon sighed, "is that Hart just called us from New York's International Airport. He says that Sandbar bailed out of his Sky Bus flight somewhere over the Rocky Mountains!" "Damn!" Unger exclaimed, "Now it's back to square one!"

Chapter 22

When Queasy left Sam's, Mizzou and Yelverton moved to a more favored place at the bar. "You know that animals live by territorial imperative, Big Guy," Mizzou told Yelverton, "and just look at you. You've come to roost upon your favorite perch, haven't you? My fine feathered friend." "Birds of a feather flock together," Yelverton mocked, flapping his arms. "Hey Sam! How's about letting us dip our beaks here with a brewski or two!"

Shoving an ice-cold, foaming schooner Yelverton's way, O'Blarney replied, "One for the money, two for the show, three to get ready, let's have your dough." "And a Vichy water, for Big Bird," Yelverton added. "Seems he can't roost without wetting his whistle."

Both quenched man-sized thirsts. Drinking into the wee hours, both became resolved to thinking that when the straight truck was finally reconditioned--and that work could be completed in one or two days--then they must advertise, or pound the pavement, or do whatever it took to get jobs.

"What we might well do is flood the neighborhood shopping malls with flyers, Yelverton," Mizzou brain stormed. "It's a basic marketing strategy, actually--and dirt cheap. We'll have some clever hand bills done to include our business name, phone number, maybe our names and, of course, our prices. Then we just walk through parking lots putting our flyers on windshields. Now what could be cheaper--or faster?" "Uh, how about one of those airplanes that buzzes the city pulling a banner behind it, Mr. Marketing Genius?" Yelverton razzed. "Yeah, right. At a hundred bucks per hour, who's going to pay for that add blitz?" Mizzou snapped, finishing his sparkling water, then ordering another. "No, seriously, Yelverton," Mizzou rambled, "you'll like the easy, low-cost approach to the campaign that I just described. I used it myself many times before, and it works." "Who's going to buy me a knew pair of boots to replace the ones that I wear out distributing those so-called flyers?" Yelverton wondered. "The exercise will do you good,"

Mizzou replied. "Huh? With your know how, you'll find a way to distribute those blurbs from your motorcycle anyway. How lazy can you get!"

"Ah advertising! One of my favorite topics," a friendly voice said. "Without advertising, the free-enterprise system does not dance. Advertising is the voice that lets capitalism sing sweet songs!" Mizzou recognized the voice. He heard it before. He focused on the face. The features were sharp, and friendly. Smiling like some long lost relative returned for a family reunion, the man extended his hand to shake Mizzou's.

"Thornberry N. Teaberry," he said, "and we have met before." Pumping Mizzou's arm vigorously he added, "Actually, it was several days ago. We talked the night away. My, the conversation was brisk and thought provoking. Was it not?" "You bet," Mizzou countered. Pointing to Smythe sitting in the corner, drinking hot coffee, he added, "I hope you'll excuse him, but he's about three sheets to the wind. If inebriation were a sail, old Smythe would be half way to Hawaii by now. He was here that night too, but wouldn't recall it now. Say, Thornberry, shake hands with John Yelverton. He's my business partner."

Extending a hand to shake Yelverton's Teaberry beamed, "A real pleasure, sir, to press the flesh, so to speak, with the true entrepreneurial spirit of this great country. Entrepreneurs are the backbone of small business anywhere, and small business is the central nervous system of our economy. If big business, mega corporation for want of another name, is the heart of enterprise, then small business is its life's blood. You are the pump that fuels economics!"

"Well, I like to think that I do work hard," Yelverton agreed, his chest swelling with new found pride, "and I do know my way around the garage. There ain't a valve job that I ain't done; an engine I ain't tuned. You name it, I've overhauled it; painted it; tuned it up, or torqued it down. Shoot. I sleep at five-hundred rpms!"

Teaberry broke into mild laughter. "Yes, indeed. But more important than the idea is the action. I can see that you two have a good thing going...a very good thing. With your combined talents, your brain and brawn, success is only to happen. I don't see how your formula can fail. Which leads me to this question." Teaberry used his powers of suspense to masterfully manipulate situations. With his right hand resting upon his chin he puzzled, "Just what did you say your exact business was?"

Yelverton started to respond but was upstaged by Mizzou. Laughing mildly he explained, "We're in the trucking business you might say. We bought a straight truck from Fly By Night Van Lines at the bankruptcy auction. We picked it up for next to nothing. Big John has refurbished it from the ground up. All that needs doing now is to find someone to use us."

"Ah, very interesting," Teaberry replied. I might just know someone who could use your services."

"Oh, really," Yelverton said, reaching for his schooner of beer. "Samuel, bring this gentleman a drink on the business, and I'll have another too." O'Blarney looked puzzled but, beer drawn from the tap, shoved a frosty foamer Yelverton's way. Then he poured coffee for Teaberry. "Oh, put it on my tab, will you Samuel?" Yelverton bubbled. "You know, Samuel, For The Birds Trucking!" "Yeah, for the birds alright!" O'Blarney cried. "Those little cheap skates already owe me nineteen bucks!" Slapping a twenty on the bar Yelverton huffed, "Here, my good beertender. The tab, and then some, for your trouble." "Gee," Sam praised sarcastically, "the last of the big spenders. Thanks!"

    While nursing his drink, Mizzou and Yelverton watched Teaberry with great anticipation. Finally, between sips, Thornberry N. Teaberry spoke. "I was just in here the other day, and Mr. O'Blarney was good enough to tell me a little bit about you, through a very colorful account of the storied history of Fly By Night's agency here in San Francisco. You see, I am a retired astronomer. As you might know, I returned to locate my darling sister and her fine, fine husband. Well," he paused, wiping a tear from his eye, "sis was adopted, but we were always close. She died recently; before I could locate her. But I did find my brother-in-law living in some shabby walk-up near Haight-Ashbury. To make a long story short, I'm retired and he's a widower. I always hoped to travel, and he hoped to return to Nevada. My sister was little people, and my brother-in-law is little people too. They had an act that they used for Circus Circus in Las Vegas. He's all that I have left in this crazy old world, so we're moving that way. Would you be interested in moving the two of us there? My few things are stored at his place, and he does not have much to move either. Just a few small items."

"Move you to Vegas? You bet!" Yelverton blurted. "We charge eighty bucks an hour to include riding time that starts the minute we leave the warehouse." "Yeah, we're interested," Mizzou bubbled. "When are you moving, anyway?" "How soon can we move?" Teaberry asked. "My brother-in-law has nothing keeping him here, nor have I." "The sooner the better, then," Yelverton said. "Just give me another day or so, Monday at the latest, and we're rolling." "Uh, I'll take that to mean Monday, then," Teaberry said, finishing his coffee, and extending his hand again for Yelverton to shake. "Mister, you've got yourself a deal!" Big John burst, vigorously shaking Teaberry's hand. "Deal," Teaberry repeated. "Deal," Mizzou parroted, also vigorously shaking Teaberry's hand. "Deal!" all said together.

"By the way," Mizzou asked, "who is this brother-in-law of yours?" "Oh, I must apologize for failing to introduce you. He's sitting right over there, enjoying one of the house specialties. Lemon-buttered shark plank."

Approaching a table, Mizzou was mildly surprised at the tiny man who stood up in the booth.

106

Extending his small hand for Mizzou to shake, he said, "I remember you. Do you remember me? Homer Herman Katzenjammer is the name. I'll bet that you're Philip Mizzou. Right?"

Chapter 23

E. X. Queasy left O'Blarney's restaurant with mixed emotions. He had enjoyed the "finest meal ever presented him" in the bay area, but vital information still eluded him. Moving toward his golden-gate-orange Bugatti he was startled by, "Pssst! Hey you! Over here!" "What? Who is that!" Queasy demanded, "I can't see you, damn it! Come out of the shadows and address me like a civilized human being!"

The shadowy darkness presented a small figure. "Who are you?" Queasy demanded. "Do I know you?" "No, you don't know me," Smythe said, "but I understand that you want some information about that butthead Sandbar. If the price is right, I can point you in the right direction." "How do I know that you're on the level?" Queasy huffed. "You might just take the money and laugh over this!" "Buttbreath Sandbar is responsible for my unemployment, and I know some guys who are on top of the situation. I know 'cause I heard them talking. Do I get fifty bucks and tell you who to check out, or do I keep my yapper shut?"

Queasy slipped Smythe a crisp bill with Ulysses S. Grant's picture, got information, and squealed his tires leaving O'Blarney's lot.

E. X. Queasy parked his Bugatti roadster in the Club A-Go-Go lot, and banged violently on the door. The last patrons were long gone, but Queasy noticed a cherry-red pick-up truck, complete with gun rack, parked in the back, so he thought that someone might be home. He looked at his wrist watch. It read 4:44 a.m. "Open up I say!" Queasy bellowed, rattling the reinforced-steel door, sending reverberations throughout the neighborhood that echoed obnoxiously into the night.

"I say there! Is anybody home?" Peeping from a porthole cut into the door, Knuckles admonished his unwanted guest. "Listen buster!..." he barked, only to stop short and say, "Oh, it's youse. I forgot that youse said this morning after closing. I wouldn't have left the door unlocked anyhow. A man can't be too careful, even though this is a respectable neighborhood. I'm just finishing the receipts for the day. Another big haul. Whenever Pandora performs, the crowds flood the joint. Drinks flow like water, and all the employees benefit. The bartenders make out, the bar maids make out; even the other dancers get bigger tips. She's a star. No doubt about it. Some day I'll own a joint and she's my head liner. I'll have her name in lights from here to Reno. I'm gonna own a string of these strip clubs, and Pandora will be my partner."

"Yes, uh, very interesting indeed, my friend. Does she know this yet?" Queasy asked, passing Knuckles slowly and only sharing common ground to smooth ruffled feathers--he loathed Knuckles. "I'll tell her when the time is right, youse can bet on that," Knuckles sighed. "A guy who has plans can always hope. She's crazy about me," he lied. "It's just that she wants everything to be perfect, youse know. She has high standards. I think that's 'cause she went to college. Some of the girls say that she's smart as a whip. But she dances like an angel. Who cares about her head," he sighed again, "when she has the figure of a goddess."

"Uh, yes indeed. That she has. That she has," Queasy agreed, setting the tone for his business proposal. "Now, Knuckles," he said, "this is the rest of the business deal that I have for you. There is something very important to me that I must recover. An associate of mine, a Philibert Sandbar, with Fly By Night Van Lines, moved some very rare and valuable property from Europe...actually Zurich, Switzerland. Well, I have a feeling that he kept this valuable property for his own benefit, wanting to profit at my expense. I can't have that!" he suddenly fumed, slamming his palm on the chrome table top, sending a whaaam echoing about the empty club.

"Yeah, well, don't bust a gut, friend," Knuckles

said with irritation. "I told youse already that I can help. Want me to step on some faces and get this property back?" "No! No!" Queasy blurted. Taking a deep breath he exhaled calmly, and replied, "Finesse. We'll use finesse. Here's the address of a garage near the warehouse where a couple of Sandbar's employees work. Someone at a tavern near there said that I might learn something by dropping in during business hours. So here is what you are to do. Go over there tonight and hang around. Be very low key. Hide out back and peek through the window if need be, but don't get caught, or we might never get this property back. Do you understand?"

"Youse bet," Knuckles agreed, "leave it to me. By the way, what about my money?" "When you come back with exhibit A, or at least information leading to its return, I'll give you five-hundred dollars. How's that?" Queasy smiled. "That'll do," is all Knuckles said.

"Now here is how you handle it," Queasy began, pointing to the brightly-polished table top with a chubby finger. "Tomorrow night, these two ex-Fly By Nighters will be working on their truck see..."

Chapter 24

"Oh, my aching head!" Yelverton complained to Mizzou, "I swear that I'll never touch another drop of alcohol so long as I live!" "Yeah, right!" Mizzou chided, "And I intend to join alcoholics anonymous tomorrow!" "Well," Yelverton continued, "I'll not touch another drop when I have to work! Say, what time is it anyway, Mizzou?" "About four minutes later than the last time you asked," Mizzou snapped. "Which makes it exactly four forty-four p.m. Okay?" "Yeah, okay, Mr. Teetotaler. Just you wait until you overdose on Vichy water and get a carbonated hangover. Boy, will I let you have both barrels!" "I can hardly wait," Mizzou guffawed. "I warned you about your evil ways." He sarcastically added, "You know that Carrie Nation was an idol of mine!"

"Yeah, well how's about carrying that wrench over my way so's I can finish this tune up. No worky no chop-chop," Yelverton frowned. Handing over the wrench Mizzou offered, "And no more beerskis for the big thirst, either. Say, what's this?" he asked, picking up a block of metal about the size of a small brick. "Oh, just some piece of bric-a-brac that I found stuffed underneath the front seat of one twenty-three. You know some drivers. There are about three more from what I can tell. Somebody probably ripped them off, then forgot that they were there. They make good wedges for engine work and exhaust repair, but otherwise, I wouldn't give you a plug nickel for any of 'em as decorations."

Rubbing much grease from one bar, Mizzou's curiosity was aroused, yet neither man observed the hulking figure lurking in shadows just outside the garage. The massive figure was not a graceful picture, trying hard to move toward light cast from the window, without tripping through a very cluttered, and potentially noisy, yard. Finally, the hulking, brooding presence nestled against the cinder-block wall: With left eye barely visible through grimy glass, he spied upon unsuspecting subjects.

"Say, we may have something here," Mizzou said. His enthusiasm building, he stammered, "Wait, wait, wait just one, dirty-doggone minute here, Big Guy! Yelverton, look at this!" "Oh, don't bust your buttons, Mizzou, you've seen plenty of phoney-baloney bric-a-brac around here! Royal bullfeathers! You lived knee deep in it with that Unger malarkey. What's so special about this junk." "This!" Mizzou cried, disturbed by Yelverton's skepticism. "Lookey here a minute. If this is what I think it is, then all of my questions are answered. What do you know about engraving?"

"I had a girl friend once who gave me a silver plated fountain pen with my initials on it," Yelverton drawled, seemingly stumped by the question. "You're close, but no cigar. No. I mean what do you think of when you see engraving like this on a plate, grease for brains. Think!" "Well, I don't know about you, but in high school I once won a pie-eating contest. My award was a personally engraved pie tin. It was none too shabby!" Yelverton gushed. "You know how much effort it takes to eat thirteen lemon-meringue pies at one sitting? Man, I almost lost it!"

"Yelverton, you have lost it!" Mizzou barked, throwing the plate against an oil drum. "Think hard, now. Engraving? Four plates? Sandbar? E. X. Queasy? Zurich, Switzerland? International shipments. Get the picture?" "Oh, yeah," Big John beamed, convinced that he finally put two and two together. "Sandbar was running contraband past customs, using Fly By Night to avoid paying duty tax."

Mizzou's frown turned to a smile and he guffawed, "No! Nice try, but you strike out in the bottom of the ninth, with the bases loaded, and two out! Now here's the idea." "Okay, Charlie Chan, I'm all ears," Yelverton said sarcastically, sitting his massive frame upon an oil drum. "The floor is yours."

"It seems obvious, actually. Elementary, at this point in time. I haven't all the facts yet, but it does seem that these four plates are used to counterfeit currency. Look at the fronts and backs of these two." "Looks like a fifty dollar bill to me," Yelverton responded. "Right!" Mizzou answered, "Now look at these." "Looks like five hundred of something or other, but I forgot my Latin, professor," Yelverton mocked.

"That's French, you know," Mizzou sighed. "You see, these are plates for American and French currency: In fifty dollar, and five-hundred franc denominations. Neither counterfeit easily, but I think French francs are more difficult than dollars to copy. What I'm saying is that Sandbar and Queasy were in to more than just drugs, Big Guy. We hit the jackpot! If these are phony plates, then Sandbar was up to his eyeballs in funny money, and probably allowed Queasy to use him to smuggle God knows what else. Now it's a cinch he flew the coop. If Queasy didn't bump him off that is. From this point forward, let's be real careful how we do business, and with whom we do it. Chances are, more than the DEA is waiting for someone to goof. The treasury gets involved with these capers."

"Are you saying, then, that Sandbar's ass is grass?" Yelverton beamed, playing the barrel upon which he sat like a bongo drum. "What's more than that, I'm saying that Sandbar's ass is on fire," Mizzou blurted, "but I wouldn't bother to pee on him to put it out!"

"Well, Big John smiled, "Sandbar can cry me a river with his troubles. But that son of a bitch always lands on his feet. He could fall off the top of the TransAmerica Building, land in a dumptruck of cow chips, and walk away smelling like a rose. I swear that that guy leads a charmed life. He has the proverbial nine lives, plus!"

"Well, all good things must come to an end. Still, we need to cover our butts," Mizzou cautioned. "Let's turn these plates over to SFPD the first chance we get. I'm not so sure just having them in our possession is legal." "Yeah, we'll do that, but first let's take care of numero uno," Yelverton said proudly. "If we don't finish one twenty-three, we don't have a truck to move Teaberry and Katzenjammer. The paint job will only take a couple of hours, and we'll let it dry naturally. What time did you tell Teaberry we'd be there, anyway?"

"I forgot to give him an exact time," Mizzou replied. "I have Teaberry's address and telephone number. We'll merely call him first thing in the morning for directions to their place. It's a piece of cake!"

The hulking figure outside the garage bulged at the eyeballs spying the bars that Mizzou and Yelverton talked over. Knuckles knew immediately that these were the objects Queasy paid him the bounty to capture. Moving with the grace of a charging bull, he gambled that he could barge into the garage, catch everyone off guard, and snatch his prize. Unfortunately, Knuckles did not see the puddle of grease that reached from the dirt yard and scooped him into its black mass. "Yeooow!" the bungling burglar cried, skidding into a pile of old oil cans. Craaash! Dozens of stacked cans spilled in noisy protest about the yard.

Barely upon his feet, Knuckles changed his course of action and stumbled toward the street, reaching his red pick-up truck before Big John Yelverton and Philip Mizzou rushed into the darkness. "Stop where you are!" Yelverton demanded, the moment Knuckles started the truck

115

and roared from the scene. "Stop, or I'll shoot!" Mizzou added melodramatically. Both looked incredulously at the other. Mizzou rubbed more grease from the bar that he still held. Raising an eyebrow he asked, "Now what do you think of phoney-baloney bric-a-brac, Big Guy?"

Chapter 25

Monday morning's golden glow of California sunshine warmly greeted Mizzou and Yelverton. Both saw fit to spend the night at the garage; mostly to protect their business interest from thieves like Knuckles, but also to assure that they would leave on time for the Katzenjammer-Newberry move. Yelverton labored most of the night putting the finishing touches on straight-truck #123. With paint dry-to-the-touch, he seemed satisfied that the job was well done, though didn't know it when he said during those wee hours, "My man, this is our crowning achievement, lookey this," that Mizzou was dead to the world--curled up in a pile of fluffy, comfortable furniture pads.

Without fanfare, then, his restoration of #123 was complete. He kicked some furniture pads into a corner, and sat down to finally admire his work.

Leaning back against this makeshift bed, he fell fast asleep. Restoration work truly was exhausting.

Both slept comfortably for several hours, wheezing and snoring like two lumberjacks, buzz sawing through Giant Sequoias. They maintained this for awhile, then, at seven thirty, were roused by a sharp bam, bam, bam on the garage door.

"Hello! Hello! Is anybody home?" a shrill voice cried. "Hello! I have something very important to tell you! Hello!" "Huh? What in thundering, blue blazes is all that commotion?" Mizzou yawned, while gazing at his wristwatch before jumping to his feet to run Yelverton and to shake him vigorously. "Big Guy! Wake up!" Mizzou pleaded. "We should have been at Katzenjammer's by now. This is one hell of a note. Our very first job and we're late!"

"Oh, don't tell me it's time to wake up and smell the coffee!" Yelverton complained. "That reminds me. I bought breakfast the last time. It's your turn this morning." "Forget feeding your face for once in your life, Big Guy!" Mizzou admonished, "If we don't get our butts in gear...!"

"Hellooo!" the voice insisted. I have some very important...!" "Oh, shut up already! I'm coming! I'm coming!" Mizzou blurted, scratching his backside while walking slowly to the door.

With very loud claaang, he rattled the metal chain that raised a rolling door, inviting bright sunlight to blind Yelverton and him, finally ending vampire-like sleep. With arm shielding his eyes

Mizzou stammered, "Yeah, yeah, yeah. What is it? What do you want at this hour of the day?" "My name is Penelope Bach and I have some information that will interest you very much!" she insisted. "Do you have the time and desire to hear me out, or what?" "Yeah, sure," Mizzou replied. "But understand that we're working men, and we should be some place an hour ago...so make it short and sweet! Huh?"

Yelverton was struck by the woman's beauty but, even more so, the familiarity of her face. He asked, "Haven't we met somewhere before? Maybe another time or another place? You're a goddess, sent down from Olympus to guide us through life. Right?" She laughed and snapped sardonically, "Not quite, bozo. You might have caught my act at Club A-Go-Go, though. I'm also known as Pandora." She smiled softly, "Ever catch my act?" The two "Easy Movers" looked at one another and said simultaneously, "Pandora Boxxe!" "Right. But, again, my real name is Penelope Bach. My friends call me Penny. Okay?" "Yeah, sure, anything you say," Mizzou said warmly. "But, again. What do you want?" "Maybe we should sit down for this," Penelope Bach warned. "You might not believe what I have to tell you." "At this point in time, I might believe anything!" Yelverton blurted, firing up his blow torch to heat water for coffee.

She began, "Well, it all started a long time ago actually, but more recently, events have been such that everything exploded." Bach grew more excited while she spoke, almost not spitting her words out quickly enough. "You see, last night, late, I was...," "Calm down and slow down," Mizzou ordered. "Tell us what you want to say, but think before you speak, and measure each word carefully...as if your life depended upon it!" Bach laughed. "My life just might depend upon it! You see last night I overheard something that involves the guy that used to own the furniture warehouse...uh, uh..." "You must mean old Fibber Sandbar himself," Yelverton spat. "He's in the news a lot lately it seems!" "Uh, yeah. That name's very familiar, indeed," Bach said coyly. "Anyway," she sighed, "it seems that he has this partner, a very fat partner at that, who wants desperately to find him and recover some very valuable property. He was telling some bozo bouncer named Knuckles all about it. In fact, he sent Knuckles over here last night to get whatever it is that's so valuable."

Mizzou and Yelverton looked at one another. Without speaking, Mizzou walked to the four plates and carried them to show Bach. "Is this what they want, do you think?" Mizzou said, his long, lean body casting a giant shadow that blocked Bach's light, so that she could not tell what he held. "Let me see, I...hand one over and I'll hold it to the light," Bach replied. "Oh, my, that's heavy!" she exclaimed. "Say. What are these, anyway? Boat anchors!"

"Not by a long shot! Look very closely--very closely indeed!" Mizzou exclaimed, "And you'll be right to think that E. X. Queasy would kill for these!" "What? I hardly know how to express this," Bach stammered. "But now everything is forming a big picture. These look like plates for fifty dollar bills, American; and the others...I'm not expert but..."

"Right you are! Par le vous Francais, mademoiselle?" Yelverton blabbed, "I was just telling my partner last night that we have captured four sets of plates for funny money!" Mizzou rolled his eyes, looked toward the ceiling, mumbled something, but otherwise did not speak. "You see," Yelverton bragged, "you have to know your international currency, and also the fine points of counterfeiting, to realize that fifty dollar and five-hundred franc denominations are favorite numbers for counterfeiting artists to make."

With this, Mizzou broke back into the conversation. "He's right. Those denominations are easily passable, so a favorite target of scam artists who bilk businesses, banks and, generally, the public, of millions of dollars annually. We know now about E. X. Queasy. From what you're telling us, Sandbar fits perfectly into the puzzle too. Probably, he skipped with a lot of bad paper that Queasy wants back. But since he can't recover the phony cash, then surely Queasy wants the plates. And by the way, thanks for warning us about lunkhead. He was here late last night, pretty near getting what he came for, 'cept something scared him off."

"That's what I rushed over here to tell you, of course," Bach sighed. "Knuckles is a ruthless enforcer, and meaner than a grizzly bear. He beats up football players from the local college just for kicks and grins." "I remember him!" Yelverton drawled. "He don't scare me!" "Yeah," Mizzou added, "there's more than one way to deal with a bully!" "You don't understand," Bach cautioned, "Knuckles is very dangerous! He has a deal with...with...," "Queasy," Mizzou said. "Yeah, Queasy," she parroted. "Anyway, they are coming to get the plates, and they're loaded! Knuckles carries a gun!"

"That does change our thinking somewhat," Mizzou said, "but we'll go for it anyway! We've come too far to turn back now. We'll contact SFPD and let them handle this." "Well, good buddy," Yelverton said. "I hate to be the bearer of bad news, but we'll loose the Katzenjammer-Newberry job if we don't get our act together."

"Oh, right! The move!" Mizzou exclaimed. "Let's get the hell over there and load him up. Is the truck ready?" "Rough and ready!" Yelverton barked. "Okay," Mizzou said, moving toward the rig, "you're the Van Captain; so you drive. Let's go!" "What about me?" Bach asked. "You can't just leave me here after I've tipped you about

Queasy and Knuckles. If they find out, they'll kill me!" "Climb aboard, then," Mizzou ordered. "You've just been drafted into the services of For The Birds Trucking!"

Chapter 26

Aloysius Saxon ruffled some papers at his desk, picked up his coffee cup, took a deep draw of the hot, black liquid, and prepared to spend another quiet day playing administrative catch-up. Just when he thought that he had it made, Commander Zelman Unger breezed into the office and blurted, "Saxon, put your walking shoes on, boy, we have us a tempest in a teapot that's a boiling caldron, and is about to overflow!" "What do you mean, Commander?" Saxon asked, his expression souring with disappointment.

Unger was full of information. He released it with great relish, for he had pulled administrative strings. In the doing, he upstaged Saxon's effort. By pulling rank, the Commander re-established himself as central figure at DEA headquarters. "Now here's the idea," Unger began, pacing nervously, looking at times like a cat about to spring on a mouse. "Saxon, after you told me about the Queasy deal, then about Sandbar crashing and burning, I thought what the hell, if we have to start from square one, we'll start with this Queasy fellow, uh, I mean Jean-Luc La Pierre. Anyhow, getting to the point, see, I got on the horn and dialed up Interpol. They tell me that our man is wanted all over Central Europe, not just France. Belgium wants him, The Netherlands wants him, Luxembourg wants him, Switzerland wants him too. Seems he's left a stinking trail all over those countries passing his bogus French francs. An Inspector Truman NuttTruffle has been hunting him big time. They know La Pierre as The Elephant, for his photographic memory--never forgets a thing once memorized. Inspector NuttTruffle tells me that their operation to bag La Pierre is called TREE, which is acronym for Trumpeting Royal Elephant Exhaust. I understand, too, that his trademark automobile is one of a kind or something."

"I did some research on that car, Commander," Saxon quicky said. "Actually, there were fewer than eight Bugatti Royale Coupe Napoleons ever manufactured. They are virtually priceless, and are known for splashy coloring, avant garde styling, a solid-chrome, horseshoe-styled grill, plus a silver hood ornament, oddly, I think, of a dancing elephant. There are other styles of Bugattis called Type Thirty-fives, Forty-ones, and Fifty-sevens, but they're not so rare--yet only five thousand plus

Bugattis were ever manufactured. We have that homing devise secured to his undercarriage but, believe me, with the splashy coloring of that classic, and the unique styling, we can't loose the guy. He sticks out like a diamond in a coal bin."

"Yeah, well that's great," Unger enthused, "because Inspector NuttTruffle is arriving this morning at San Francisco International Airport to extradite Monsieur Jean-Luc La Pierre, also known as Dr. E. X. Queasy, to The Hague, Netherlands, where international law shall throw the book at him! And I fully expect that we'll receive the French Foreign Legion Medal of Honor if we don't step all over ourselves trying to impress one another with brilliant strategy. Get my drift, Sarge?"

Saxon looked at the floor and swallowed hard, just when Zzyzzx walked up and handed Commander Unger a steaming cup of black coffee. "We'd better be getting a move on, Commander," Zzyzzx suggested. "Remember that Inspector NuttTruffle left Sunday morning after talking to you. His flight is due to arrive anytime. You know how those time zones always screw me up. He might be standing there right now waiting for us. We really shouldn't be late. That's rude, you know."

"Yeah, yeah, yeah...I know, I know," Unger blabbed. "Now, listen, Sarge. I want you to park your ego. No bickering with Zzyzzx, here, and no brown nosing NuttTruffle. I happen to know now that he was your contact in Interpol, but believe you me, he only wants TREE buzz sawed, so lets not create a logjam in the river of valor and hog all the credit, glory, honor, and praise for ourselves. We are not to be made laughing stocks by those Big Kahunas at the federal offices in Washington, by bungling this operation. Get my drift?"

Saxon took another long swallow of black coffee. He looked at Zzyzzx from the corner of his eye, then said sarcastically, "No problem, Commander. Right now I'll settle for being a goody-two-shoes-team player and, who knows, maybe we'll all get that Legion Medal of Honor."

Chapter 27

Rumbling toward Katzenjammer's home, up and down San Francisco's steepest streets--let alone California's steepest streets--Mizzou and Yelverton, with their rider, Penelope Bach, did not notice an exotic roadster following safely far behind. E. X. Queasy and his henchman, Knuckles, were hell-bent-for-leather determined to recover the prize. They breezed along comfortably, the four counterfeit plates safely stored in an old, unused, emergency-flares box that Mizzou chose for its handle, and sturdy metal nature. He spoke. "We've got to do something about those plates, you know, Yelverton. I'm telling you, this all makes perfect sense now. More than SFPD will be interested in the nature of our business. At least the Treasury Department, and who knows what other bureaus, will crawl out of the woodwork for this caper."

"Yeah, your right, my man," Yelverton agreed. "But like I said before; first things first. We'll take care of business, and if we have time left over, then we'll turn those plates over to the law. Anyhow, if they're as important as you say, any lawman can handle the paperwork for us. Right?"

"I happen to know factually that when you have counterfeited material, the United States Treasury, in concert with the Secret Service, responds in these matters," Bach said. "So yeah, just about any police agency can take the evidence, then initiate an investigation, until the appropriate federal authority acts. Usually a regional agent responds on behalf of Washington."

"Wow!" sounds like mighty cloak and dagger stuff to me!" Yelverton beamed, gulping coffee directly from his thermos. Do you think we'll get our pictures in the newspaper over all this, or, better yet, collect a reward for our trouble?"

"If we're lucky, we won't get our butts shot off by that fat man and his hired gorilla," Mizzou sighed. "But, hey, lets keep our eye on the road. Hey, wait, slow down! According to the directions that Teaberry gave me, we're to turn right at the next traffic light, then take a right at the stop sign, and from there, go one-half block or so to the walk-up row of apartments that Katzenjammer moved into." He gulped to catch his breath. "I for one will be glad to get them loaded and us on the open road, Big Guy. I figure by the map that the fastest way to Las Vegas is down Interstate Five to Los Angeles, then Interstate Ten on to Nevada. We'll jog straight into neon city that way. By the by, did you remember to rob your piggy bank so that you can play the one-armed bandits?"

"Very funny, Mr. Bigbucks," Yelverton chided, rolling to a stop in front of Katzenjammer's residence. "Let's not forget, that it was me that won the very last Giant's baseball pool at O'Blarney's. Who's the dean of gamblers here, anyway? Me!" he burst proudly, thumb pointed to his swelling chest. "I've forgotten more about rolling the dice, and lady luck, than you'll ever know!"

"Oh, Las Vegas!" Bach exclaimed. "I've always wanted to visit there. You boys simply must include me in your plans. Please! I might even find work there as a chorus girl. I'll come back for my personal effects after all this blows over," she added coyly.

Mizzou and Yelverton just looked at one another. Finally, Mizzou said, "Yeah, sure. But first things first. Let's give our plan of action to the customer, then we'll worry about the other business."

The sleek, exotic Bugatti Royale Coupe Napoleon, with the silver, trumpeting-elephant, hood ornament, glowed brilliant orange under beaming California sunshine. Pulling the right hand drive vehicle to the curb, The Elephant looked to his henchman and said, "We won't make our move here. There's too much traffic, pedestrian and vehicular, to bring attention to us. We'll bide our time, then strike at the first opportunity along the way. I happen to know from my source at O'Blarney's, uh, Smythe, that these birdbrains are moving this load to Las Vegas. We'll have plenty of chances to waylay those pigeons and get our goods."

Queasy did not tell Knuckles any more than he thought necessary to do the job. He hired muscle, not intelligence. "Further, he added, "I see that the plot thickens with that, that fan dancer along. What in the world is she doing with them, anyway?"

Knuckle's hair bristled at the nape of his neck. He was extremely jealous of Pandora--her paying attention to any other man was something he could not deal with. "Youse never know about the scumbag Johns that come into the place. I remember kicking those twos' butts once before over her! I figure she knows them from Club A-Go-Go, and maybe she is having them move her or something." Knuckles scratched his head. Finished talking, he snapped open the cylinder of his Smith & Wesson, snub-nose, .38-caliber revolver, to ensure that all six cartridges were chambered. Snapping the cylinder back into place, he stuffed the weapon into his belt, then stared balefully toward straight-truck #123.

Teaberry greeted the "Easy Movers" at the front door, but Yelverton spoke first. "Got to apologize for being late, but there was this hellish traffic jam on Highway One O'One," he lied. We would have been here an hour ago, but traffic stood still. There was an accident, I guess." Wanting to sound like Mizzou, he concluded, "Unavoidable circumstances, you know."

"Don't worry about a thing," Teaberry reassured them. "Homer and I have everything packed and ready to go. We have this first floor apartment, so the only steps are down to the truck. And you may recall, Philip, that he hasn't that much anyway. Shouldn't take all that long to load and be on our way. We're really playing this 'by-the-ear,' anyhow, so time is not a big factor. I'm just glad as hell to see you!"

"Great," Mizzou replied. "And by the way, TNT, this is Penelope Bach. She's along for the ride if you don't object." "Object? Why should I object?" he asked. "We can always stand the company of a beautiful lady any old time." Smiling broadly, and extending her hand for him to shake, Penelope Bach told Teaberry, "My friends call me Penny, okay?"

"Fine with me," Teaberry replied. "Homer went

to the store for some last-minute items. He's bringing back breakfast for everyone. I hope that you don't mind Jumping Jack's Flapjacks take-out. It's the closest eatery. Their waffles and fried egg sandwiches are really pretty good!" "Hey, bring it on! Bring it on!" Yelverton blabbed. "Jumping Jack's Flapjacks is my favorite breakfast!"

"You'd eat your boots boiled in saltwater and garnished with seaweed, if you'd missed dinner the night before," Mizzou mocked. "But, yeah. Thanks for the gesture TNT. We'll do a quick inventory, have a quicker bite to eat, get you loaded up, and be on our way. Okay?"

"No problem. No problem at all," Teaberry assured them. "But allow me to add this. Homer will be back shortly, and we both agree that we want to detour from schedule. You see, I've always wanted to take in the great outdoors and behold the wonders of nature. If we take the northern route, we can reach Nevada via Highway One Twenty, and drive through the Sierra Nevadas. I understand that the scenery is really something to behold there. And nestled majestically within the Sierra Nevada range is Yosemite National Forest. The waterfall there, Yosemite Falls, is spectacular I hear, and hiking trails apron the most breathtaking valleys and vistas this side of paradise. I have heard, too, of challenging peaks and sheer cliffs in the Sierra Nevada Mountain Chain, so, if its all the same to you, and of course I'll pay for your time, what do you say?"

Mizzou and Yelverton looked at one another, shrugged their shoulders, then nodded their heads in agreement. Bach broke her silence just as Homer Herman Katzenjammer walked through the door with two big bags of Jumping Jack's Flapjacks. "What about me? Do I still factor into the equation?" she asked coyly, running her finger along Teaberry's chin. "I promise not to get in the way." "Harrrumph! Well, of course you're to go along," he replied sharply. "We wouldn't think of abandoning you!"

"We'll find something for you to do, believe me!" Yelverton beamed. "It will be great having a beautiful lady along, no matter what you do. If nothing else, just sit tight and look pretty!" Bach bristled with this comment. She purred, "Uh, yes, sugarplum. I see that chivalry and chauvinism are both alive and well and thriving in San Francisco. But beggars can't be choosers. Still, I'll earn my keep. So just point me to the nearest love seat and grab an end. You'll see that I don't just play hard. I work hard, too, big boy."

Mizzou and Yelverton wolfed down their food while loading Katzenjammer's furnishings faster than they might normally have, but for the change of plan. Bach did her best to keep up with them, but without the benefit of proper conditioning, she tired. The muscles in her back twitched spasmodically. The strength in her arms left when she tried to pick up and carry an overstuffed chair. Walking less than two feet, she dropped the heavy chair, narrowly missing Katzenjammer's foot in the process.

"Let that go, Penny," Mizzou insisted, "and take a break for pity sake! The strain is building up in your arms, back, and legs. You'll pass out from the exertion. We do this every day and you don't."

"Yeah, well, exotic dancing is no piece of cake, believe me," she insisted. "But you're right. One works a different set of muscle groups performing on stage. I think that I will take a break."

No sooner than climbing into the truck's cab, she fell fast asleep. Listening the previous night to the diabolical scheming of Queasy and Knuckles--pacing nervously while planning a course of action--kept her awake. Arriving at sunrise to bang on For The Bird's garage door, Penelope Bach was exhausted by noon, and well past her bedtime.

The last items were loaded into straight-truck #123. Slamming shut the heavy rear doors with a whaaam, Mizzou slapped dust from his hands. Climbing into the van's cab, he parked his size twenty-two, double-wide pontoons on the floor. He glanced at Bach, slumped comfortably asleep in the middle of the wide seat, then said to Yelverton, "Let's hit it, Van Captain, sir. Teaberry gave me an idea of what's ahead. We'll follow him and Katzenjammer in their car. It's that junker over there."

"What in thundering, blue blazes? What is that

thing?" Yelverton asked indignantly. "There are rules and regulations, established by the Department of Motor Vehicles, that prohibit rolling junk yards! I used to think that one twenty-three was the pits!"

Mizzou guffawed and said, "He saved a few bucks by getting a Rent-A-Bomb for the trip. Just so happens they have offices in Los Angeles and Las Vegas too, so he can drop it off there." Firing up old #123, Yelverton frowned and replied, "Yeah, drop it off there, if it doesn't drop them off along the way."

Following Teaberry's lemon-yellow, Ford Edsel Rent-A-Bomb along Highway 120, Mizzou and Yelverton did not talk to one another much. They did not mean to neglect civic responsibility by keeping the counterfeit plates too long, but between a rock and hard place to "Move Easy" or not at all, a contingency plan permitted surrendering the plates to the Las Vegas Police Department. Mizzou looked inside the box, saw the four plates safely tucked inside, slammed the lid shut and shoved them underneath the seat. Neither one observed that a bright, golden-gate-orange roadster still followed within safe distance, carrying two daring men on a desperate mission.

Chapter 28

Commander Unger, Agents Saxon and Zzyzzx, waited for hours at San Francisco International Airport, before realizing that they had missed Inspector NuttTruffle's arrival. Wondering what to do next, Commander Unger finally realized that a quick call to Europe was his only option.

Climbing into the passenger side of the front seat, he looked forlornly at Saxon behind the wheel and blurted, "I don't believe it! Interpol tells me that NuttTruffle left on schedule, but got socked in at New York's International Airport. Something about fog for crying out loud! San Francisco is the pea-soup capital of the world, and he's locked into New York! Anyway, we can't wait for him now. We know what we need to know to close operation TREE successfully, so let's tail that fat bastard...uh, I mean elephant, and be done with it! Oooh!" Unger complained, grabbing his forehead. "This piercing headache. Whenever the ships about to hit the sand, my brain scrambles. Zzyzzx, give me some of those pain killers you keep in your pocket. I have a three pill zinger!"

Pulling the drab-green, four-door, government sedan onto the freeway, Saxon whined, "We're getting behind the eight ball, Commander. While you were telephoning Europe, the blip on our screen lit up, after being idle all morning, then took off.

Seems our man Queasy is heading out of town in an easterly direction. The built-in map tells me that they're on Highway One Twenty even as I speak, so that's where we're heading."

"Far be it from me to stand in the way of progress," Unger snapped, popping the pain killers into his mouth; swallowing the bitter tablets without water. "At least he's making a move. Now we have something to sink our teeth into. Just wish Interpol were here to witness us in our glory. We'll bag this drug lord and his dirty paper!" he bragged. "There will be promotions all around after this--believe me!"

Within two hours Saxon, Unger, and Zzyzzx had a visual on the majestic Bugatti Royale. Maintaining a respectable distance, Saxon held back, per Unger's orders, settling for tracking a bleep on a screen. Queasy, meanwhile, maintained a safe distance from the bright-blue truck that chugged along Highway 120 toward Yosemite National Park. With dusk approaching, Yelverton turned the vehicle's headlights on high beam. Streaming over winding roads, through deep valleys and heavy forests, they reached Yosemite Park in total darkness.

Stopping in Yosemite Village, the "Easy Movers" joined Teaberry and Katzenjammer at the visitor's lodge for a bite to eat. They still did not spot the exotic roadster when it wheeled in shortly after their arrival. All were too busy eating. Queasy and

Knuckles got rooms and parked behind the lodge. Within minutes, Saxon drove inconspicuously by the roadster. The Teaberry party decided to "rough-it-out" in rented tents. Saxon, Unger, and Zzyzzx decided to sleep in their drab-green vehicle, but to take turns keeping an eye on Queasy.

Chapter 29

Finished gobbling their beans and franks supper, the Teaberry party ordered several thermos bottles of hot coffee to go, climbed aboard #123, and fired up the lemon-yellow Ford Edsel; driving several miles to a spot that the park ranger recommended for its breathtaking panorama of the High Sierras. All this, of course, was within view and hiking distance of El Capitan and Yosemite Falls.

Reaching Glacier Point Road, they proceeded to Glacier Point--with its 3,500 ft. elevation--pitched tents, fired up kerosene lanterns, then spent the better part of the night exchanging yarns and ghost stories about unnatural and supernatural phenomenon.

"What about all that Bigfoot legend now that

we're here, Mr. Crypto Zoologist?" Big John Yelverton chided, poking Mizzou in the ribs, then winking mischievously. "Yeah. Well, you saw the souvenir stand along Highway One Twenty the same as me, Big Guy," Mizzou replied defensively. "Just you wait. You'll see that there is a following for those big fellows. Tomorrow we'll do a little exploring and, mind you, we won't spot one o' them critters right out the shoot, but, well...you'll eat them words!"

Teaberry laughed hard. Katzenjammer curled up comfortably asleep in his tent, and Bach seemed preoccupied with other matters. She sat near the edge of Glacier Point, comfortable upon a bench, mesmerized by the brilliant light show of a googolplex of stars. "Ah, yes. Again you pique my intellectual sanctum. The Sasquatch, Bigfoot as you call it, is most legendary among the British Columbia Indian tribes, but seen everywhere throughout the Pacific Northwest. I believe, too, that its taxonomic classification is Homo Nocturnus--definitely a hominid type of anthropoid."

Yelverton looked at Mizzou and whispered, "I wish old Thorny there would speak English. What did he say?" "He means," Mizzou answered wryly, "that Bigfoot walks upright like a man, and has a lower trunk proportioned to its upper trunk--meaning that its legs are proportioned to its arms. You know that gorillas, or orangutans, for instance, have long arms but short legs." Yelverton scratched his head then whispered, "I knew that!"

Sounding like a lecture in Zoology 101, Teaberry's colorful depiction of the Sasquatch legend captivated his audience. He told of numerous sightings throughout the past one-hundred years, and even of an encounter or two. "Mostly, Sasquatch is an elusive figure, taking refuge in very remote, overgrown ranges here in the Northwest. Sasquatch travels by night and day, but its cunning is that of a wolf--a major reason that sightings, encounters, and inevitably capture, are rare. If nothing else, and I'll guarantee you this, even if we don't spot creature one, the scenery will capture your heart. Just you wait until the sun rises above the Cathedral Range--trip to the light fantastic!"

Chapter 30

Tuesday, 12:00 a.m., found Queasy and Knuckles hunched over a small conference table in the lodge's reading room, planning their next move. Saxon drank steaming coffee in the cold night air, pacing back and forth like a cougar stalking its prey. He stamped his feet hard on the asphalt parking lot, but nothing relieved the numbing cold in his toes. He cursed to himself, wondering why he was the unlucky one drawing first shift. He knew, somehow, that Zzyzzx conned him into drawing the shortest of three matchsticks that put him there. "Never trust a man named Zzyzzx," he muttered, taking too deep a draw of steaming coffee, and spilling the hot liquid down his throat and chest. He instinctively jumped back but was too late. The rush of fluid stained his goose-down, flight jacket. "Hot damn!" he spat. "Zzyzzx will pay for this!"

Queasy and Knuckles did not chat very long at their meeting. "Here's what I want you to do, Mr. Knuckles," Queasy wheezed. "First thing in the morning, see, we drive back to that souvenir stand that we passed, you know, the one with the gargantuan costume in the window, and then we give you a shot at recovering my prize peacefully. You know, by finesse and brainpower, rather than sheer muscle. You're to create the diversion, and with those birdbrains' focus elsewhere, I sneak into their camp and snatch my goods."

"Just what is it that I'm supposed to be helping youse find!" Knuckles demanded. "Youse never did tell me what's so damn hot! It isn't diamonds, or something like that, is it?" "No, nothing so exotic, or expensive, I'm afraid...but important nevertheless. Just you let me worry about what it is that we're after. Oh, by the way," he beamed, the reward I promised. Five crisp, green Benjamin Franklins for your collection. That should more than motivate you to do the job today. I want my property back desperately!"

Queasy and Knuckles finished their late night session. Shuffling to their rooms, both fell asleep fast. Saxon continued pacing and stamping through Yosemite Village, unsuccessful at staying warm. Autumn nights in northern California were very cool.

Before the sun grandly rose above Cathedral Range, Bach busied herself about the campsite, picking up what few scraps were scattered about, then disposing of them in nearby trash containers. Then she climbed aboard #123 to rummage beneath the seat. She found what she was looking for--the flare box. She looked nervously about the area, wanting to see if anyone else was up. No one was then, but Katzenjammer soon joined her, and not long after that, Teaberry and Yelverton were up--anxious to pour a thermos bottle's last drops of warm coffee.

"We must not be rude and drink all the refreshment," Teaberry warned, "lest we tempt the wrath of Philip!" "Oh, he won't mind so much, Professor," Yelverton said, teeth chattering in the cold dawn. "We're not that far out of the loop anyway." Teaberry looked quizzically at Yelverton. He did not understand. "I mean," Yelverton said, "that it's not that far a drive back to breakfast. We can all pile into your yellow bomber over there, and chow down in minutes."

"All the same," Teaberry replied, screwing the cap back onto the thermos to keep the last cup warm, "you can take the man out of civilization, but you can't take the civilization out of man. Now can you? We aren't barbarians!"

Yawning, stretching--his long, willowy arms eagle's wings in cold air--Mizzou greeted all others. "Don't mind if I do, thank you. Coffee is just what I had in mind. Say, Big Guy, while we have the floor, let's show TNT our strongbox, you know, the very special plates that we've almost forgotten."

"You show him, my man," Yelverton replied. "It's your baby now." Penelope Bach said quickly, "I'll get them," before Mizzou had the opportunity to do so. She ran to the front seat of the van, and reached underneath, needing both hands to tote the box back.

"Very interesting. Very interesting, indeed!" Teaberry exclaimed, examining the goods. "If I'm not mistaken, these are very fine counterfeit plates." The weight of them was not lost on him either. "But the weight of these bars! My word! They're heavy as bricks! We must hand these over to the proper police agency as soon as possible. We'll have the Park Rangers' Office notify the California Highway Patrol. If nothing else, they can take possession, do the paperwork, and turn these rather remarkable but totally bogus plates, over to whomever. Don't you all agree?"

"Fine by me. How about you, Big Guy? Big Guy!" Mizzou caught Yelverton off guard--being distracted by the magnificence of sunrise throughout the valley. "Mizzou, just lookey at that orange baby! I didn't think the sun could ever be more grand than over The City! Zounds, Mizzou, it looks like ten million orange groves exploding!"

"I warned you that your heart would immediately be captured by it all, didn't I?" Teaberry bragged. "You know we ought to form a hiking party before breakfast. We don't need to go far...just far enough to wet our appetites. How about it?"

They hiked, yet before long, Bach begged off, complaining of sore muscles from the previous day. Teaberry, Katzenjammer, Yelverton, and Mizzou did walk on, determined to hike at least one mile before driving to the village for breakfast. No one knew that a sleek, exotic roadster pulled quietly onto the road's shoulder, just a bend away from Glacier Point.

"Don't bungle this now, Mr. Knuckles," Queasy implored. "All you have to do is sneak up, just giving them a glimpse...a glimpse of you, and they'll be off, chasing you to kingdom come. I'll sneak into their camp, get what I have to get, then meet you back here, and we're home free. Got it?"

"Yeah, got it," Knuckles frowned. "But I feel so stupid in this monkey suit. And it itches! Not to mention the stink!" "That's a genuine Bigfoot replica, I'll have you know," Queasy scolded, "and the guy there wouldn't take any less than five crisp, Benjamin Franklins for it, so this caper is not cheap. But forget that. Now get out there and do your thing!"

Wherever Queasy went, the DEA surely followed. Cruising past his Bugatti, The Elephant tried to ignore the G-men, instead glancing at the timepiece mounted in the middle of his steering wheel, noting that Knuckles was gone some fifteen minutes. He finally looked at the drab-green vehicle with its three passengers, but recognized none. He thought that maybe all tourists got up bright and early to admire the view from vantages along Glacier Point Road.

Saxon drove to the first bend past Glacier Point. Observing the bright-blue van parked near the lemon-yellow Edsel, he pulled to the shoulder of the road. "This is where I get out and try to make contact, Commander" he said. "We go with Plan A. Right? Queasy was tailing those birds from the warehouse because they must have what he wants. I'll hide by their campsite, wait for him to make his move, then you and Zzyzzx back me up. Okay?"

"Yeah, you got it, Sarge. One thing, though. No gun play if you can help it. We don't want innocent people getting their butts shot up." "Hey! Far be it from me to endanger wildlife or the human species," Saxon bubbled cheerily. For someone spitting venom only hours before, he seemed in unusually good spirts. "How did you get that stain on your jacket?" Zzyzzx asked, just before Saxon disappeared into the wood line. "Ask me no questions, and I'll tell you no lies," Saxon snapped sarcastically. Then he was gone.

Knuckles loped alongside a ridge in the general direction of the hikers. Stumbling about the trails, he fell several times before he got the hang of his costume. From a distance, he looked like the pictures of Bigfoot that Mizzou showed to Yelverton and, hamming it up, Knuckles sprang on his curled hands occasionally, thinking that a genuine Bigfoot might do same. Spotting the party of four, he gave out the most hearty yeoow, scaring the hikers completely.

Yelverton rubbed his eyes in disbelief. "Ma, ma, ma, Mizzou!" he stammered. "Over there!" Mizzou looked in the direction Yelverton pointed and, though shocked, yelled, "Follow me everyone! Bigfoot!" The chase was afoot. All took off except Teaberry, who seemed disturbed by it all. Tramping through the growth, all huffed, and all puffed, but none caught Knuckles.

Bach walked directly to the Ford Edsel and grabbed the strongbox. Sitting on the car's front seat, she shrieked in disbelief when Saxon sprang from the cover of woods to confront her. Sargie-O, baby!" she cried. "You scared me to death!" "What have you there?" he demanded. "Are those the gold bars?" "Huh, uh, sure. You know that I was only putting them up for safe keeping until you got here. The economy might be the pits, but I wouldn't stiff you. You know that!" "Yeah, well. Queasy is just around the corner. Those gold bars of his are worth a mint. Probably two or three million on the trading block. We can't be too careful."

Climbing into the Edsel, he shoved Penelope Bach to the driver's side. "We have what we wanted all this time. Now let's get the hell gone!"

"I wouldn't be too footloose and fancy-free with other people's money, my fine feathered friends," a voice said. Walking from the woods, E. X. Queasy brandished a snub-nosed, .38-caliber revolver. "It's been a long time, indeed, waiting and tracking; asking and calculating. I knew, sooner or later, that I would come face to face with the party responsible for my grief. It was you, wasn't it Miss Pandora and whoever you are, that ripped me off?"

Motioning with the revolver, Queasy walked to the passenger side and slid next to Saxon." "Here's what we're to do," he ordered. "First, fire this contraption up, then drop me off at my Bugatti. It's waiting around the bend." Bach started the car's engine by working the gas pedal, sending bulbous clouds of noxious exhaust into the cool morning air. She also worked the brakes, noticing that they were mushy. "Enough! Enough, already!" Queasy cried, coughing smoke.

"No, indeed. That will be quite enough from

you," another voice ordered. "Drop that weapon and, all of you, out of the car. Now!" Teaberry meant business. He was cool as a cucumber. He brandished a .45-caliber Smith & Wesson. Unfortunately, Bach did not see or hear him. She continued revving the car's engine. Working the brakes, they still felt soft. Her plan was to stomp on the gas and crash into a tree--assuring escape.

But when she engaged the shifter, Knuckles stormed into camp, loping along with the unnatural grace of a bogus Bigfoot. "Jumping Jehoshaphat! What is that?" she shrieked, slamming the shifter into reverse and stomping on the gas pedal. Bach only thought that the car was in drive. Panic stricken by Bigfoot, confused in reverse, she meant to brake, not accelerate. The Ford Edsel, backfiring, veered wildly backwards, crashing through the guardrail at Glacier Point, before falling 3,500 ft. to the canyon floor below. "Helllp!" they cried pathetically.

Penelope Bach, a.k.a. Pandora Boxxe, the queen of burlesque, Aloysius Saxon, the cop's cop, and Jean-Luc La Pierre, a.k.a. E. X. Queasy, the quintessential con-artist counterfeiter, were sentenced by nature--sent screeching and screaming to an uneasy rest--three rogues who crashed and burned for the love o' gold.

Following close behind Knuckles, Katzenjammer, Mizzou, and Yelverton reached camp in concert with Teaberry picking up Queasy's discarded snub-nosed, .38-caliber–then holding the rampaging, bogus ape-man at bay. "What's up Inspector NuttTruffle? Ooops!" Katzenjammer sighed. "I didn't mean to spill the beans." Mizzou and Yelverton looked incredulously at one another.

"Not to worry," TNT said as the drab-green sedan pulled into camp. "It's almost over anyway. Allow me to introduce myself." He smiled at Commander Zelman Unger and Agent Zzyzzx when they climbed from their car. "I am Inspector Truman NuttTruffle of Interpol. These are my credentials. I have extradition papers for Jean-Luc La Pierre, as well as the recovery of four bars of gold and, finally, the return of one Bugatti Royale Coupe Napoleon, valued at approximately eight million dollars. Unfortunately, Mr. La Pierre lies colder than a mackerel on canyon floor below. But, I'll arrange for the return of his personal effects, err filchings, for the courts to adjudicate. If you'll arrest that Sasquatch imposter," NuttTruffle sighed, pointing to Knuckles, "I'll declare this case closed."

"Come on, you big gorilla," Zzyzzx barked, slapping handcuffs upon the hulk. "It's bread and water time, Baby Huey!"

Chapter 31

Wednesday morning's sun rose gloriously golden over the Sierra Nevada Mountains, crowning Yosemite National Park's Tuolumne Canyons majestically. "I'm still not sure that I get the big picture, Inspector NuttTruffle," Mizzou said, dunking a jelly donut into a steaming cup of black coffee with one left wing. "You were preoccupied yesterday doing all the administrative things that police do. Now that we're leaving, how's about filling us in on the juicy details."

"Well," NuttTruffle sighed, "it's all rather sad, actually. A long time ago, Interpol realized that bogus money was circulating throughout Central Europe. We knew that our man was La Pierre, we only needed to catch him red-handed. That's when operation TREE sprang up. La Pierre/Queasy moved back and forth from Zurich to San Francisco so much and, with such ease, we figured that he had big-time, uh....help. Birds of a feather flock together you know. Not coincidentally, your man Sandbar, who was shipping drugs through Zurich, connected with La Pierre/Queasy. That's where your Drug Enforcement Agency came in. I established a telephone rapport with Aloysius Saxon through a Harry Hart. They were monitoring Sandbar. But the more we tried to nail La Pierre, the harder it became, so I flew here weeks ago, undercover of course, to see what was wrong. I suspected a leak from the top. Realizing La Pierre's penchant for flash and intrigue, and his historic clever disguise of wealth, I figured that he somehow planted a lot of gold in those shipments of furniture. He's done it before. And because of the problems, I figured someone else knew about his modus operandi at this end--hence the credibility gap. Sooner or later, this mole would rear an ugly head, and I intended to be there to pounce. Your Pandora was working as an operative for Saxon--called him Sargie-O. They schemed all along to steal that gold, just as soon as they found it. By the by, that day you freaked out moving La Pierre/Queasy, Yelverton unwittingly used those bars to block the tires of his truck. La Pierre/Queasy kept them well in sight, amongst the greasy trappings of his garage. Sometimes the obvious is the best place you know. But Yelverton had no clue the Pandora's box he opened. Those brownies that you ate contained truth drugs--sodium pentothal. In his angst, Dr. E. X. Queasy was desperate to stash the gold into his Bugatti Royale, and ship the whole kit and caboodle together. When Sandbar came along and complicated matters by firing Yelverton, he did that because La Pierre/Queasy complained. But it didn't get the gold back. Apparently Smythe stuffed the bars under the front seat of the truck and forgot about them.

Smythe helped me a lot...saw him crying in his beer one day at O'Blarney's. He told me everything--even introduced me to Homer

Katzenjammer."

"But how did Queasy, uh, I mean La Pierre find us?" Mizzou puzzled. "He had lots of help from me actually," NuttTruffle replied. "I even had Smythe pass information to him at O'Blarney's last Saturday night. Smythe cornered La Pierre in the parking lot."

"That's incredible," Mizzou sighed. "Never a dull moment at Fly By Night. I'll sure miss that place." NuttTruffle laughed, "You realize of course, that most of those moves were monitored by DEA. Aloysius Saxon, Zelman Unger, Zzyzzx, even Penelope Bach, played parts in the moves."

"Bach was Mrs. Unger. Right?" Yelverton beamed proudly. "I just knew there was something strange about her!" "Bingo!" NuttTruffle laughed again. "Even with all that make-up, there's no fooling an expert on women, now is there?"

Walking toward the Bugatti Royale Coupe Napoleon NuttTruffle said, "Would you mind driving Homer back to his city digs? He wasn't really moving, he only co-operated to help bait the trap. Of course, your time for the past forty-eight hours will be billed to operation TREE." "At eighty smackers per hour?" Yelverton blabbed. "That's for a van and two men you know. The furniture game ain't all that easy!"

Starting the golden-gate-orange Bugatti Royale--with its Fort Knox-gold, winged fenders--NuttTruffle mumbled, "Whatever you say,

Mr. Yelverton. Whatever you say." Pointing dancing-elephant-hood-ornament west, and trumpeting the regal horn, Inspector NuttTruffle rolled sleekly from the parking lot.

"Well, what now, Mizzou?" Yelverton asked, removing his pork-pie cap to scratch his head and to stare at El Capitan rising mightily in the distance. "As long as we're here, let's take in the sights, Big Guy," Mizzou replied.

"Yeah," Katzenjammer said. "We have Yosemite Falls, El Capitan, Giant Sequoias, and who knows how many hiking trails to discover. The game is afoot! I feel like another challenge!" Katzenjammer thumped his chest mightily. "Nothing like crisp, mountain air to bring out the beast in a man." Mizzou cackled, "Yeah, who knows, and if we're lucky, we might even spot us a Bigfoot. To Bigfoot!" he yelled. "To Bigfoot!" all yelled back. Bouncing about canyon walls "Tooo Biiigfooot!" echoed in refrain.

Three "Easy Movers," fearless still, then wallowed about fresh mountain air, basking beneath those golden-morning sunbeams, that back dropped the purple-mountain majesty of Sierra Nevada's Cathedral Range, atop glorious northern California.